THE HEART OF A GENTLEMAN

ONLY FOR LOVE (BOOK 1)

ROSE PEARSON

THE HEART OF A
GENTLEMAN

CHAPTER ONE

"Thank you again for sponsoring me through this Season." Lady Cassandra Chilton pressed her hands together tightly, a delighted smile spreading across her features as excitement quickened her heart. Having spent a few years in London, with the rest of her family, it was now finally her turn to come out into society. "I would not have been able to come to London had you not been so generous."

Norah, Lady Yardley smiled softly and slipped her arm through Cassandra's.

"I am just as glad as you to have you here, cousin." A small sigh slipped from her, and her expression was gentle. "It does not seem so long ago that I was here myself, to make my Come Out."

Cassandra's happiness faded just a little

"Your first marriage was not of great length, I recall." Pressing her lips together immediately, she winced, dropping her head, hugely embarrassed by her own forthrightness "Forgive me. I ought not to be speaking of such things."

Thankfully, Lady Yardley chuckled.

"You need not be so concerned, my dear. You are right to say that my first marriage was not of long duration, but I *have* found a great happiness since then - more than that, in fact. I have found a love which has brought me such wondrous contentment that I do not think I should ever have been able to live without it." At this, Cassandra found herself sighing softly, her eyes roving around the London streets as though they might land on the very gentleman who would thereafter bring her the same love, within her own heart, that her cousin spoke of. "But you must be cautious," her cousin continued. "There are many gentlemen in London – even more during the Season – and not *all* of them will seek the same sort of love match as you. Therefore, you must always be cautious, my dear."

A little surprised at this, Cassandra looked at her cousin as they walked along the London streets.

"I must be cautious?"

Her cousin nodded sagely.

"Yes, most careful, my dear. Society is not always as it appears. It can be a fickle friend." Lady Yardley glanced at Cassandra then quickly smiled - a smile which Cassandra did not immediately believe. "Pray, do not allow me to concern you, not when you have only just arrived in London!" She shook her head and let out an exasperated sigh, evidently directed towards herself. "No doubt you will have a wonderful Season. With so much to see and to enjoy, I am certain that these months will be delightful."

Cassandra allowed herself a small smile, her shoulders relaxing in gentle relief. She had always assumed that London society would be warm and welcoming and, whilst there was always the danger of scandal, that danger came only from young ladies or gentlemen choosing to behave improperly. Given that she was quite determined *not* to behave so, there could be no danger of scandal for her!

"I assure you, Norah, that I shall be impeccable in my behavior and in my speech. You need not concern yourself over that."

Lady Yardley touched her hand for a moment.

"I am sure that you shall. I have never once considered otherwise." She offered a quick smile. "But you will also learn a great deal about society and the gentlemen within it – and that will stand you in good stead."

Still not entirely certain, and pondering what her cousin meant, Cassandra found her thoughts turned in an entirely new direction when she saw someone she recognized. Miss Bridget Wynch was accompanied by another young lady who Cassandra knew, and with a slight squeal of excitement, she made to rush towards them – somehow managing to drag Lady Yardley with her. When Cassandra turned to apologize, her cousin laughingly disentangled herself and then urged Cassandra to continue to her friends. Cassandra did so without hesitation and, despite the fact it was in the middle of London, the three young ladies embraced each other openly, their voices high with excitement. Over the last few years, they had come to know each other as they had accompanied various elder siblings to London, alongside their parents. Now it was to be their turn and the joy of that made Cassandra's heart sing.

"You are here then, Cassandra." Lady Almeria grasped her hand tightly. "And you were so concerned that your father would not permit you to come."

"It was not that he was unwilling to permit me to attend, rather that he was concerned that he would be on the continent at the time," Cassandra explained. "In that regard, he was correct, for both my father *and* my mother have taken leave of England, and have gone to my father's properties on the continent. I am here, however, and stay now with my cousin." Turning, she gestured to Lady Yardley who was standing only a short distance away, a warm smile on her face. She did not move forward, as though she was unwilling to interrupt the conversation and, with a smile of gratitude, Cassandra turned back to her friends. "We are to make our first appearances in Society tomorrow." Stating this, she let out a slow breath. "How do you each feel?"

With a slight squeal, Miss Wynch closed her eyes and shuddered.

"Yes, we are, and I confess that I am quite terrified." Taking a breath, she pressed one hand to her heart. "I am very afraid that I will make a fool of myself in some way."

"As am I," Lady Almeria agreed. "I am afraid that I shall trip over my gown and fall face first in front of the most important people of the *ton*! Then what shall be said of me?"

"They will say that you may not be the most elegant young lady to dance with?" Cassandra suggested, as her friends giggled. "However, I am quite sure that you will have a great deal of poise – as you always do – and will be able to control your nerves quite easily. You will not so much as stumble."

"I thank you for your faith in me."

Lady Almeria let out a slow breath.

"Our other friends will be present also," Miss Wynch added. "How good it will be to see them again – both at our presentation and at the ball in the evening!"

Cassandra smiled at the thought of the ball, her stomach twisting gently with a touch of nervousness.

"I admit to being excited about our first ball also. I do

wonder which gentlemen we shall dance with." Lady Almeria swiveled her head around, looking at the many passersby before leaning forward a little more and dropping her voice low. "I am hopeful that one or two may become of significant interest to us."

Cassandra's smile fell.

"My cousin has warned me to be cautious when it comes to the gentlemen of London." Still a little disconcerted by what Lady Yardley had said to her, Cassandra gave her friends a small shrug. "I do not understand precisely what she meant, but there is something about the gentlemen of London of which we must be careful. My cousin has not explained to me precisely what that is as yet, but states that there is much I must learn. I confess to you, since we have all been in London before, for previous Seasons – albeit not for ourselves – I did not think that there would be a great deal for me to understand."

"I do not know what things Lady Yardley speaks of," Miss Wynch agreed, a small frown between her eyebrows now. "My elder sister did not have any difficulty with *her* husband. When they met, they were so delighted with each other they were wed within six weeks."

"I confess I know very little about Catherine's engagement and marriage," Lady Almeria replied, speaking of her elder sister who was some ten years her senior. "But I *do* know that Amanda had a little trouble, although I believe that came from the realization that she had to choose which gentleman was to be her suitor. She had *three* gentlemen eager to court her – all deserving gentlemen too – and therefore, she had some trouble in deciding who was best suited."

Cassandra frowned, her nose wrinkling.

"I could not say anything about my brother's marriage, but my sister did wait until her second Season before she accepted a gentleman's offer of courtship. She spoke very little to me of any difficulties, however - and therefore, I do not understand what my cousin means." A small sigh escaped her. "I do wish that my sister and I had been a little closer. She might have spoken to me of whatever difficulties she faced, whether they were large or small, but in truth, she said very little to me. Had she done so, then I might be already aware of whatever it is that Lady Yardley wishes to convey."

Miss Wynch put one hand on her arm.

"I am sure that we shall find out soon enough." She shrugged. "I do not think that you need to worry about it either, given that we have more than enough to think about! Maybe after our come out, Lady Yardley will tell you all."

Cassandra took a deep breath and let herself smile as the tension flooded out of her.

"Yes, you are right." Throwing a quick glance back towards her cousin, who was still standing nearby, she spread both hands. "Regardless of what is said, I am still determined to marry for love."

"As am I." Lady Almeria's lips tipped into a soft smile. "In fact, I think that all of us – our absent friends included – are determined to marry for love. Did we not all say so last Season, as we watched our sisters and brothers make their matches? I find myself just as resolved today as I was then. I do not think our desires a foolish endeavor."

Cassandra shook her head.

"Nor do I, although my brother would have a different opinion, given that he trumpeted how excellent a match he made with his new bride."

With a wry laugh, she tilted her head, and looked from one friend to the other.

"And my sister would have laughed at us for such a

suggestion, I confess," Lady Almeria agreed. "She states practicality to be the very best of situations, but I confess I dream of more."

"As do I." A slightly wistful expression came over Miss Wynch as she clasped both hands to her heart, her eyes closing for a moment. "I wish to know that a gentleman's heart is filled only with myself, rather than looking at me as though I am some acquisition suitable for his household."

Such a description made Cassandra shudder as she nodded fervently. To be chosen by a gentleman simply due to her father's title, or for her dowry, would be most displeasing. To Cassandra's mind, it would not bring any great happiness.

"Then I have a proposal." Cassandra held out her hands, one to each of her friends. "What say you we promise each other – here and now, that we shall *only* marry for love and shall support each other in our promises to do so? We can speak to our other friends and seek their agreement also."

Catching her breath, Lady Almeria nodded fervently, her smile spreading across her face.

"It sounds like a wonderful idea."

"I quite agree." Miss Wynch smiled back at her, reaching to grasp Cassandra's hand. "We shall speak to the others soon, I presume?"

"Yes, of course. We shall have a merry little band together and, in time, we are certain to have success." Cassandra sighed contentedly, the last flurries of tension going from her. "We will all find ourselves suitable matches with gentlemen to whom we can lose our hearts, knowing that their hearts love us in return."

As her friends smiled, Cassandra's heart began to soar. This Season was going to be an excellent one, she was sure.

Yes, she had her cousin's warnings, but she also had her friends' support in her quest to find a gentleman who would love her; a gentleman she would carry in her heart for all of her days. Surely such a fellow would not be so difficult to find?

CHAPTER TWO

"*I* should like to hear something... significant... about you this Season."

Jonathan rolled his eyes, knowing precisely what his mother expected. This was now his fourth Season in London and, as yet, he had not found himself a bride – much to his mother's chagrin, of course. On his part, it was quite deliberate and, although he had stated as much to his mother on various occasions, it did not seem to alter her attempts to encourage him toward matrimony.

"You are aware that you did not have to come to London with me, Mother?" Jonathan shrugged his shoulders. "If you had remained at home, then you would not have suffered as much concern, surely?"

"It is a legitimate concern, which I would suffer equally, no matter where I am!" his mother shot back fiercely. "You have not given me any expectation of a forthcoming marriage and I continually wonder and worry over the lack of an heir! You are the Marquess of Sherbourne! You have responsibilities!"

Jonathan scowled.

"Responsibilities I take seriously, Mother. However, I will not be forced into–"

"I have already heard whispers of your various entanglements during last Season. I can hardly imagine that this Season will be any better."

At this, Jonathan took a moment to gather himself, trying to control the fierce surge of anger now burning in his soul. When he spoke, it was with a quietness he could barely keep hold of.

"I assure you, such whispers have been greatly exaggerated. I am not a scoundrel."

He could tell immediately that this did not please his mother, for she shook her head and let out a harsh laugh.

"I do not believe that," she stated, her tone still fierce. "Especially when my *dear* friend, Lady Edmonds, tells me that you were attempting to entice her daughter into your arms!" Her eyes closed tight. "The fact that she is still willing to even be my friend is very generous indeed."

A slight pang of guilt edged into Jonathan's heart, but he ignored it with an easy shrug of his shoulders.

"Do you truly think that Lady Hannah was so unwilling? That I had to coerce her somehow?" Seeing how his mother pressed one hand to her mouth, he rolled his eyes for the second time. "It is the truth I tell you, Mother. Whether you wish to believe me or not, any rumors you have heard have been greatly exaggerated. For example, Lady Hannah was the one who came to seek *me* out, rather than it being me pursuing her."

His mother rose from her chair, her chin lifting and her face a little flushed.

"I will not believe that Lady Hannah, who is so delicate a creature, would even have *dreamt* of doing such a thing as that!"

"You very may very well not believe it, and that would not surprise me, given that everyone else holds much the same opinion." Spreading both hands, Jonathan let out a small sigh. "I may not be eager to wed, Mother, but I certainly am not a scoundrel or a rogue, as you appear to believe me to be."

His mother looked away, her hands planted on her hips, and Jonathan scowled, frustrated by his mother's lack of belief in his character. During last Season, he had been utterly astonished when Lady Hannah had come to speak with him directly, only to attempt to draw him into some sort of assignation. And she only in her first year out in Society as well! Jonathan had always kept far from those young ladies who were newly out – even, as in this case, from those who had been so very obvious in their eagerness. No doubt being a little upset by his lack of willingness, Lady Hannah had gone on to tell her mother a deliberate untruth about him, suggesting that *he* had been the one to try to negotiate something warm between them. And now, it seemed, his own mother believed that same thing. It was not the first time that such rumors had been spread about gentlemen – himself included and, on some occasions, Jonathan admitted, the rumors had come about because of his actions. But other whispers, such as this, were grossly unfair. Yet who would believe the word of a supposedly roguish gentleman over that of a young lady? There was, Jonathan considered, very little point in arguing.

"I will not go near Lady Hannah this Season, if that is what is concerning you." With a slight lift of his shoulders, Jonathan tried to smile at his mother, but only received an angry glare in return. "I assure you that I have no interest in Lady Hannah! She is not someone I would consider even stepping out with, were I given the opportunity." Protesting his innocence was futile, he knew, but yet the words kept coming. "I do not even think her overly handsome."

"Are you stating that she is ugly?"

Jonathan closed his eyes, stifling a groan. It seemed that he could say nothing which would bring his mother any satisfaction. The only thing to please her would be if he declared himself betrothed to a suitable young lady. At present, however, he had very little intention of doing anything of the sort. He was quite content with his life, such as it was. The time to continue the family line would come soon enough, but he could give it a few more years until he had to consider it.

"No, mother, Lady Hannah is not ugly." Seeing how her frown lifted just a little, he took his opportunity to escape. "Now, if you would excuse me, I have an afternoon tea to attend." His mother's eyebrows lifted with evident hope, but Jonathan immediately set her straight. "With Lord and Lady Yardley," he added, aware of how quickly her features slumped again. "I have no doubt that you will be a little frustrated by the fact that my ongoing friendship with Lord and Lady Yardley appears to be the most significant connection in my life, but he is a dear friend and his wife has become so also. Surely you can find no complaint there!" His mother sniffed and looked away, and Jonathan, believing now that there was very little he could say to even bring a smile to his mother's face, turned his steps towards the door. "Good afternoon, Mother."

So saying, he strode from the room, fully aware of the heavy weight of expectation that his mother continually placed upon his shoulders. He could not give her what she wanted, and her ongoing criticism was difficult to hear. She did not have proof of his connection to Lady Hannah but, all the same, thought poorly of him. She would criticize his close acquaintance with Lord and Lady Yardley also! His friendships were quickly thrown aside, as were his explanations and his pleadings of innocence - there was nothing he could say or do that would bring her even a hint of satisfaction, and Jonathan had no doubt that, during this Season, he would be a disappointment to her all over again.

"Good afternoon, Yardley."

His friend beamed at him, turning his head for a moment as he poured two measures of brandy into two separate glasses.

"Sherbourne! Good afternoon, do come in. It appears to be an excellent afternoon, does it not?"

Jonathan did so, his eyes on his friend, gesturing to the brandy on the table.

"It will more than excellent once you hand me the glass which I hope is mine."

Lord Yardley chuckled and obliged him.

"And yet, it seems as though you are troubled all the same," he remarked, as Jonathan took a sip of what he knew to be an excellent French brandy. "Come then, what troubles you this time?" Lifting an eyebrow, he grinned as Jonathan groaned aloud. "I am certain it will have something to do with your dear mother."

Letting out an exasperated breath, Jonathan gesticulated in the air as Lord Yardley took a seat opposite him.

"She wishes me to be just as you are." Jonathan took a small sip of his brandy. "Whereas I am less and less inclined to wed myself to *any* young lady who has her approval... simply because she will have my mother's approval!"

Lord Yardley chuckled and then took a sip from his glass.

"That is difficult indeed! You are quite right to state that *you* will be the one to decide when you wed... so long as it is not simply because you are avoiding your responsibilities."

"I am keenly aware of my responsibilities, which is precisely *why* I avoid matrimony. I already have a great deal of demands on my time – I can only imagine that to add a wife to that burden would only increase it!"

"You are quite mistaken."

Jonathan chuckled darkly.

"You only say so because your wife is an exceptional lady. I think you one of the *few* gentlemen who finds themselves so blessed."

Lord Yardley shrugged.

"Then I must wonder if you believe the state of matrimony to be a death knell to a gentleman's heart. I can assure you it is quite the opposite."

"You say that only because you have found contentment," Jonathan shot back quickly. "There are many gentlemen who do not find themselves so comfortable."

Lord Yardley shrugged.

"There may be more than you know." He picked up his brandy glass again. "And if that is what you seek from your forthcoming marriage to whichever young lady you choose, then why do you not simply search for a suitable match, rather than doing very little other than entertain yourself throughout the Season? You could find a lady who would bring you a great deal of contentment, I am sure."

Resisting the urge to roll his eyes, Jonathan spread both hands, one still clutching his brandy, the other one empty.

"Because I do not feel the same urgency about the matter as my mother," he stated firmly. "When the time is right, I will find an excellent young lady who will fill my heart with such great affection that I will be unable to do anything but look into her eyes and find myself lost. *Then* I will know that she is the one I ought to wed. However, until that moment comes, I will continue on, just as I am at present." For a moment he thought that his friend would laugh at him, but much to his surprise, Lord Yardley simply nodded in agreement. There was not even a hint of a smile on his lips, but rather a gentle understanding in his eyes which spoke of acceptance of all that Jonathan had said. "Let us talk of something other than my present situation." Throwing back the rest of his brandy, and with a great and contented sigh, Jonathan set the glass back down on the table to his right. "Your other guests have not arrived as yet, I see. Are you hoping for a jovial afternoon?"

"A cheerful afternoon, certainly, although we will not be overwhelmed by too many guests today." Lord Yardley grinned. "It is a little unfortunate that I shall soon have to return to my estate." His smile faded a little. "I do not like the idea of being away from my wife, but there are many improvements taking place at the estate which must be overseen." His lips pulled to one side for a moment. "Besides which, my wife has her cousin to chaperone this Season."

"Her cousin?" Repeating this, Jonathan frowned as his friend nodded. "You did not mention this to me before."

"Did I not?" Lord Yardley replied mildly, waving one hand as though it did not matter. "Yes, my wife is to be chaperoning her cousin for the duration of the Season. The girl's parents are both on the continent, you understand, and given that she would not have much of a coming out otherwise, my wife thought it best to offer."

Jonathan tried to ignore the frustration within him at

the fact that his friend would not be present for the Season, choosing instead to nod.

"How very kind of her. And what is the name of this cousin?"

"Lady Cassandra Chilton." Lord Yardley's gaze flew towards the door. "No doubt you will meet her this afternoon. I do not know what is taking them so long but, then again, I have never been a young lady about to make her first appearance in Society."

Jonathan blinked. Clearly this was more than just an afternoon tea. This Lady Cassandra would be present this afternoon so that she might become acquainted with a few of those within society. Why Lord Yardley had not told him about this before, Jonathan did not know – although it was very like his friend to forget about such details.

"Lady Cassandra is being presented this afternoon?"

His friend nodded.

"Yes, as we speak. I did offer to go with them, of course, but was informed she was already nervous enough, and would be quite contented with just my dear wife standing beside her."

Jonathan nodded and was about to make some remark about how difficult a moment it must be for a young lady to be presented to the Queen, only for the door to open and Lady Yardley herself to step inside.

"Ah, Lord Sherbourne. How delighted I am to see you."

With a genuine smile on her face, she waved at him to remain seated rather than attempt to get up to greet her.

"Good afternoon, Lady Yardley. I do hope the presentation went well?"

"Exceptionally well. Cassandra has just gone up to change out of her presentation gown – those gowns which the Queen requires are so outdated and uncomfortable! She will join us shortly."

The lady threw a broad smile in the direction of her husband, who then rose immediately from his chair to go towards her. Taking her hands, he pressed a kiss to the back of one and then to the back of the other. It was a display of affection usually reserved only for private moments, but Jonathan was well used to such things between Lord and Lady Yardley. In many ways, he found it rather endearing.

"I am sure that Cassandra did very well with you beside her."

Lady Yardley smiled at her husband.

"She has a great deal of strength," she replied, quietly. "I find her quite remarkable. Indeed, I was proud to be there beside her."

"I have only just been hearing about your cousin, Lady Yardley. I do hope to be introduced to her very soon." Shifting in his chair, Jonathan waved his empty glass at Lord Yardley, who laughed but went in search of the brandy regardless. "You are sponsoring her through the Season, I understand."

His gaze now fixed itself on Lady Yardley, aware of that soft smile on her face.

"Yes, I am." Settling herself in her chair, she let out a small sigh as she did so. "I have no doubt that she will be a delight to society. She is young and beautiful and very well-considered, albeit a little naïve."

A slight frown caught Jonathan's forehead.

"Naïve?"

Lady Yardley nodded.

"Yes, just as every young lady new to society has been, and will be for years to come. She is quite certain that she will find herself hopelessly in love with the very best of a gentleman and that he will seek to marry her by the end of the Season."

"Such things do happen, my dear."

Lady Yardley laughed softly at Lord Yardley's remark, reaching across from her chair to grasp her husband's hand.

"I am not saying that they do not, only that my dear cousin thinks that all will be marvelously well for her in society and that the *ton* is a welcoming creature rather than one to be most cautious of. I, however, am much more on my guard. Not every gentleman who seeks her out will be looking to marry her. Not every gentleman who seeks her out will believe in the concept of love."

"Love?" Jonathan snorted, rolling his eyes to himself as both Lord and Lady Yardley turned their attention towards him. Flushing, he shrugged. "I suppose I would count myself as someone who does not believe such a thing to have any importance. I may not even believe in the concept!"

Lady Yardley's eyes opened wide.

"You mean to say that what Lord Yardley and I share is something you do not believe in?"

Blinking rapidly, Jonathan tried to explain, his chest suddenly tight.

"No, it is not that I do not believe it a meaningful connection which can be found between two people such as yourselves. It is that I personally have no interest in it. I have no intention of marrying someone simply because I find myself in love with them. In truth, I do not know if I am even capable of such a feeling."

"I can assure you that you are, whether or not you believe yourself to be."

Lord Yardley muttered his remark rather quietly and

Jonathan took in a slow breath, praying that his friend would not start instructing him on the matter of love."

Lady Yardley smiled and gazed at Jonathan for some moments before taking a breath and continuing.

"All the same, I do want my cousin to be cautious, particularly during this evening's ball. I want her to understand that not every gentleman will be as she expects."

"I am sure such gentlemen will make that obvious all by themselves."

This brought a frown to Lady Yardley's features, but a chuckle came from Lord Yardley instead. Jonathan grinned, just as the door opened and a young lady stepped into the room, beckoned by Lady Yardley. A gentle smile softened her delicate features as she glanced around the room, her eyes finally lingering on Jonathan.

"I feel as though I have walked into something most mysterious since everyone stopped talking the moment I entered." One eyebrow arching, she smiled at him. "I do hope that someone will tell me what it is all about!"

Jonathan rose, as was polite, but his lips seemed no longer able to deliver speech. Even his breath seemed to have fixed itself inside his chest as he stared, his mouth ajar, at the beautiful young woman who had just walked in. Her skin was like alabaster, her lips a gentle pink, pulled into a soft smile as blue eyes sparkled back at him. He had nothing to say and everything to say at the very same time. Could this delightful young woman be Lady Yardley's cousin? And if she was, then why was no one introducing him?

"Allow me to introduce you." As though he had read his thoughts, Lord Yardley threw out one hand towards the young woman. "Might I present Lady Cassandra, daughter to the Earl of Holford. And this, Lady Cassandra, is my dear friend, the Marquess of Sherbourne. He is an excellent sort. You need have no fears with him."

Bowing quickly towards the young woman, Jonathan fought to find his breath.

"I certainly would not be so self-aggrandizing as to say that I was 'an excellent sort', Lady Cassandra." he was somehow unable to draw his gaze away from her, and his heart leaped in his chest when she smiled all the more. "But I shall be the most excellent companion to you, should you require it, just as I am with Lord and Lady Yardley."

There was a breath of silence, and Jonathan cleared his throat, aware that he had just said more to her than he had ever said to any other young lady upon first making their acquaintance. Even Lord Yardley appeared to be a little surprised, for there was a blink, a smile and, after another long pause, the conversation continued. Lady Yardley gestured for her cousin to come and sit beside her, and the young lady obliged. Jonathan finally managed to drag his eyes away to another part of the room, only just becoming aware of how frantically his heart was beating. Everything he had just said to his friend regarding what would occur should he ever meet a young lady who stole his attention in an instant came back to him. Had he meant those words?

Giving himself a slight shake, Jonathan settled back into his chair, lost in thought as conversation flowed around the room. This was nothing more than an instant attraction, the swift kick of desire which would be gone within a few hours. There was nothing of any seriousness in such a swift response, he told himself. He had nothing to concern himself with and thus, he tried to insert himself back into the conversation just as quickly as he could.

CHAPTER THREE

"*Y*ou have done very well today."

Cassandra gave her cousin a wry smile.

"You need not say such things if your only intention is to ease my nerves. I know my face must have been very red indeed when I curtsied to the Queen, such was my nervousness!"

Lady Yardley laughed softly as the carriage continued on its way.

"I speak honestly, although yes, your cheeks were a little rosy, but that is to be expected! What is important is that you were presented to the Queen, and all went very well. The afternoon tea was a joy and you have taken everything in your stride. You appeared poised and genteel and amiable throughout the entire afternoon. At the ball, you will be much the same and thus, it will go very well indeed."

Cassandra nodded her thanks, seeing that her cousin was genuine.

"I appreciate all you have said. My doubt comes from the fact that one gentleman appeared very disinterested in my conversation."

Lord Yardley's smile began to fade as he glanced at his wife.

"Lord Sherbourne appeared most disinterested in me. I did attempt to speak with him but he showed very little interest in anything I had to say." A slight nudge of fear tried to fill her heart but she ignored it, pushing it down as Lady Yardley reached out to squeeze her hand. "What if other gentlemen are as he was?"

"I would say that Lord Sherbourne was not himself this afternoon." Lady Yardley glanced at her husband, who then nodded. "For whatever reason, he seemed quite disinclined to *all* conversation, not just your own."

Cassandra glanced from her cousin to Lord Yardley and back again, wondering whether Lady Yardley spoke the truth, or if she was merely attempting to make Cassandra feel better. Lord Yardley, however, was frowning and nodding slowly, one finger running over his chin and that gave her the impression that what Lady Yardley had said was quite true.

"His mood did seem to change once some of the other guests had arrived," Lord Yardley admitted quietly. "I had not thought of that until you mentioned it, my dear. But yes, Lord Sherbourne did not appear to be at all inclined towards conversation. Therefore, I would not take it as a personal slight, Lady Cassandra." Lord Yardley grinned suddenly. "That is, unless every other gentleman this evening ignores you and you will then find yourself in such a difficulty, you will not know which way to turn!"

"Yardley!" Lady Yardley exclaimed, clearly upset over his mock teasing, but Cassandra only laughed, thinking Lord Yardley the most amiable gentleman, and glad indeed that her cousin had found such happiness.

"I am sure you know that I am only jesting," Lord

Yardley clarified, hastily, although his lips were still upturned in a smile. "I would not have you take Lord Sherbourne's silence personally. I am sure it had nothing to do with you." His eyebrows lifted for a moment. "In fact, now that I recall, I am able to inform you that Lord Sherbourne has had something else to contend with."

"Indeed?" Lifting one eyebrow, Lady Yardley kept her gaze trained on her husband. "Lord Sherbourne has always given the impression of being a very contented fellow, with very few troubles at all. What is it that he now struggles with?"

Interested in the answer to what her cousin had asked, Cassandra dropped her gaze to her hands, feigning indifference. She could not keep her interest from growing, however, for Lord Sherbourne had changed in a most noticeable manner – since he had been seemingly glad to converse with her at first, and thereafter had become very silent.

"You know very well that I have no intention of telling you anything." Lord Yardley laughed, reaching to take his wife's hand. "Although I suppose I am meant to have no secrets from you, so I find myself in quite a dilemma."

Lady Yardley leaned forward, her smile sending a sparkle to her eyes.

"Tell me a little, my dear husband."

Lord Yardley grinned, his expression softening. Catching the look shared between husband and wife, Cassandra looked away, warmth flushing her cheeks. This was the sort of intimacy that she longed for in her own life. Their love for each other was clearly the source of their happiness, and Cassandra could not help but be a little envious.

"I shall speak carefully, then," Lord Yardley continued

in a teasing manner. "And remind you, my dear Lady Yardley, that Lord Sherbourne has a mother still living. And that *he* remains unmarried."

At this, Lady Yardley giggled and shook her head, her eyes sparkling.

"I believe you have told me everything you can," she remarked with a smile. "And I am sorry for Lord Sherbourne and his difficult situation."

Cassandra too found herself smiling – albeit more from relief than anything else! From Lord Yardley's brief explanation, she now understood that Lord Sherbourne was having some difficulties with his mother. Cassandra assumed that the gentleman was being hounded to marry, for was that not what every mother longed for? Cassandra could understand that, even if, as it seemed, Lord Sherbourne did not.

"Does Lord Sherbourne have no desire to wed then?" As both Lord and Lady Yardley exchanged a look, Cassandra frowned slightly, wondering at the exchange. "I would have thought a gentleman of his standing would require an heir."

"All in good time." Lord Yardley shrugged. "Those are Lord Sherbourne's words, you understand. No one will tell him when he is to marry, save for his own heart."

"Enough talking about Lord Sherbourne!" Lady Yardley gestured to the window. "We have arrived."

There was an excitement in Lady Yardley's voice that Cassandra did not share, such was her nervousness. Drawing in slow breaths, she sought out her courage and found that she had none. She had been presented, to the *Queen,* she told herself. Could a ball be so very different? Did it really require her to be so nervous?

Lady Yardley smiled in understanding of all that

Cassandra was feeling at present.

"Make sure that you have your dance card ready, stand by me and all will be well."

"And recall that you are not to dance the waltz this evening," Lord Yardley added, a small smile at one side of his mouth. "In the balls thereafter, you may, but tonight, you may not. But do not be afraid. It will not set you apart or make you appear any worse than any of your friends. In fact, I am sure it will make you all the more appealing to the gentlemen of the *ton*." His eyes roved towards his wife again. "It certainly did for me."

The flush in Lady Yardley's cheeks was enough to make Cassandra smile, and her nervousness began to crumble. Her cousin was quite correct, she had nothing to fear. Therefore, she would do everything to make certain that she enjoyed the ball, and that meant letting go of her anxiety and instead, allowing her thoughts to drift onto how wonderful an evening this would be. Taking a deep breath, she smiled at her cousin and then moved out of the carriage, accepting the hand of the footman as she stepped down onto the pavement.

Her first ball was about to begin.

"Two dances, Lord Fernsten?"

Cassandra's heart quickened suddenly as she looked up into Lord Fernsten's face. The gentleman was more than handsome, with a broad smile on his face that sent a flicker toward his green eyes.

"But of course, Lady Cassandra. Someone as beautiful as you must surely be offered more than one dance! I myself am the fortunate one to have been granted such a boon."

Fluttering her fan lightly in front of her face, Cassandra became all too aware of the blush which warmed her. Lord Fernsten was indeed a very amiable gentleman, clearly desirous to offer her a great many compliments.

"You are very kind. I look forward to stepping out with you."

The gentleman nodded and stepped away, leaving Cassandra to turn back to her small group of friends. There was Miss Wynch to her right, Lady Almeria to her left with Miss Madeley, Lady Elizabeth and Miss Millington coming to stand in front of her. They clustered around her, their expressions eager, and Cassandra could not help but smile.

"Did you say that Lord Fernsten wishes to dance with you on two occasions this evening?"

Cassandra nodded.

"Yes. We are to dance very soon, and then again near the end of the ball." Cassandra clasped her closed fan in both hands, close to her heart, as she drew in a long breath. "I think him quite delightful. His manner is most agreeable and to ask to dance with me twice is... very kind."

Miss Millington wrinkled her nose, although her eyes danced.

"I am afraid I cannot agree with you. I must say that Lord Stockholm is the very best of gentlemen, for he asked me to dance with him within the first few moments after my arrival! I am sure that he saw me standing a little alone from the rest and therefore, thought to shower kindness upon me."

"That was very generous, I would agree," Lady Elizabeth remarked, her eyes glowing with obvious excitement. "It seems that, thus far, we have had an excellent evening and only the first few dances have been taken! Are not all of these gentlemen quite wonderful?"

Cassandra let out a contented sigh, her hands dropping to her sides as she looked around the room. It was more than wonderful, especially now, since her dance card was already almost full! Yes, she concluded silently, there were a great many excellent gentlemen present this evening. Her brows lifted gently, a sudden idea filling her heart. Could it be that, in this room, there stood the very gentleman who might, one day, be standing by her side as her husband? Could that fellow be here this evening?

Her lips curved.

Perhaps the gentleman I shall fall in love with has spoken to me already!

The thought sent such a brilliant smile across her face that, as her gaze roved around the room, another gentleman stopped suddenly, his head twisting towards her. After a few moments, he inclined his head and Cassandra, aware of his sudden interest, nodded at him. The gentleman then began to look around the room, craning his neck this way and that, although Cassandra did not quite understand why. It was only after seeing some beckoning, gesticulating, and whispering into another gentleman's ear, that she finally understood what was happening, for when Lord Sotherton began to make his way towards her – the unknown gentleman beside him – she understood that he had been seeking an introduction.

"Lady Cassandra."

Cassandra inclined her head.

"Lord Sotherton."

The gentleman gave her a brief smile before gesturing to the other gentleman – who then stepped even closer.

"Forgive me for staring, but I simply could not *help* but seek an introduction. It has thrilled my heart to see such beauty in that smile."

All of her friends fell silent as Cassandra's fan fluttered nervously near her warm cheeks. She said nothing, for the gentleman had, truly, spoken out of turn, as they had not yet been introduced. She looked inquiringly to Lord Sotherton, who flushed, and quickly made the introductions. He did not smile, however, and instead had a heavy frown sweeping across his brow. Cassandra could not imagine what had brought such an expression to his face.

"This is the Earl of Darlington," Lord Sotherton finished, quickly, as the gentleman in question bowed.

"Lord Darlington." Cassandra sank into a curtsey, making sure that it was perfect in every way. "I am delighted to make your acquaintance. Have you been in London long?"

The gentleman's smile sent gold into his hazel eyes, the sharp planes of his cheekbones softening a little.

"I am almost always in London," he told her. "But somehow, despite being so, I have never been introduced to you!" Again, Cassandra's cheeks warmed and she fluttered her fan a little more firmly. "Might I hope that your dance card is not entirely filled, Lady Cassandra? Has fate kept one space for me, mayhap?"

A quiet giggle escaped Cassandra's mouth as she slid her dance card from her wrist and then handed it to him. The gentleman was more than eager to stand up with her and she was delighted to accept. It was a compliment of the highest order, she considered, to have been sought out in such a fashion.

"Ah, it seems fate *has* smiled on me tonight." Lord Darlington dotted his initials quickly down for the quadrille, his mouth lifting as he looked back at her. "But I see that you also have the waltz."

"Alas, I am not able to dance the waltz as yet, Lord

Darlington." Smiling a little ruefully as the gentleman's face fell, she spread her hands. "However, I shall be able to do so at future balls."

"Then I will be the first to stand up with you when you are permitted to dance the waltz, Lady Cassandra, you can be assured of that!" Cassandra giggled again, a little embarrassed at her reaction, for she did not quite know how to respond to Lord Darlington's obvious flirtations. "The quadrille will have to suffice." Lord Darlington grinned before handing her back the dance card. "Otherwise, I look forward to standing up with you for the waltz at our next opportunity, Lady Cassandra. Might I have your word on that?"

"You may," Cassandra found herself saying, without having had any intention of speaking so.

Her eyes fixed themselves on Lord Darlington as he walked across the ballroom floor, a heartfelt sigh going with him as she wondered how long it would be until she was in his arms.

"Lord Darlington appears to be interested in your company a great deal."

Cassandra opened her mouth to say that, yes, she was very glad of his interest, only to snap it closed as she noticed her cousin nearby. Lady Yardley had already warned her not to become too enamored of any particular gentleman – and to do so on the evening of her first ball *would* be foolish. Taking a breath, she set her shoulders.

"I shall be glad to dance with him, as I shall be glad to dance with any gentleman," she declared, inciting a look of surprise from Miss Madeley. "There are a great many gentlemen here I should like to dance with. I must remind myself that it would be foolish to think only of one in particular, when there are so many I am, as yet, unacquainted with."

Lady Elizabeth smiled and came to stand beside Cassandra.

"I suppose that is true – and we are all agreed on our pact to aid each other in our search for a love match, are we not?"

Cassandra smiled at her.

"Of course we are."

"Then, should one gentleman in particular catch your attention – catch *any* of our notice, we would tell one another, would we not?"

The other young ladies nodded as Cassandra did the same.

"Certainly, I would," she answered quickly. "But I can assure you all that, at this moment, I am focusing my thoughts on all of the dances I am to enjoy, praying that I shall not make a single mistake!"

A murmur of laughter ran around the group.

"I am sure you will not." Lady Almeria gestured to the center of the room. "Look, the quadrille is almost upon us, which will be your time to step out with Lord Darlington."

"While the rest of us watch with a great deal of envy," Miss Wynch put in, making Cassandra laugh.

"I am sure you shall not, for you all have your own gentlemen to dance with, do you not?" Leaning closer to Miss Wynch, she smiled. "If we are to go by how successful this ball has been, then mayhap our hopes of being wed in a love match will be fulfilled a good deal more quickly than we expected!" Her shoulders lifted in a half-shrug. "Mayhap it is something of a foolish idea, but I am sure it could be done. Perhaps we shall all be blessed enough to find a gentleman who loves us before the Season is out."

CHAPTER FOUR

"Thank you for dancing with me."

Lord Darlington reached to press her fingers as they rested on his arm, his head close to her ear, and Cassandra jumped with a little surprise. It was not common for a gentleman to be so forward.

"But of course. It was kind of you to ask me," she murmured, keeping her gaze fixed straight ahead rather than looking at Lord Darlington. She did not want him to catch any sort of flicker in her eyes, for while she might find herself a little overwhelmed by dancing with him, she certainly did not want him to know of it. Her opinion of the gentleman had altered somewhat during their dance, for he had done nothing but look around at every other guest as they had stepped out together. It did not seem to matter whether or not *she* was present and required his attention. Lord Darlington wanted only to be seen, and her presence was only to be as a support, rather than of any real worth to him.

It seems as though my first thoughts about Lord Darlington were incorrect.

"Now, you will think my question a little odd, but does your father intend to provide you with as significant a dowry as he gave your sister?"

The man's voice was loud, catching the attention of one or two others.

A cold hand grasped at Cassandra's heart, hearing the tutting of another gentleman who walked near them, who was clearly as astonished – and perhaps even as shocked – as Cassandra was by such a question. Lord Darlington did not appear to be put off, however, for his head was still turned towards her, his gaze still fixed.

"I – I think my father is a very generous man."

Lord Darlington chuckled and Cassandra's face burned.

"It is well known to the *ton* how much your father gave on the occasion of your sister's marriage. I am glad to hear that it will be much the same for you."

"I expect it to be."

Her heart began to pound. Whatever did he mean by such a question? Suddenly, the urge to remove herself from his company began to grow very strong indeed.

"What say you to stepping out for a short while to get a breath of fresh air?"

Cassandra turned her head towards his as they meandered slowly away from the center of the room, Lord Darlington's pace unhurried.

"A breath of fresh air?" she repeated as Lord Darlington nodded. "Whatever do you mean?"

Lord Darlington chuckled.

"Only to say it is very hot in this room and that the gardens are quite magnificent. There is still enough light by which we might see and there will be a few lanterns also."

Immediately Cassandra shook her head.

"I hardly think that would be appropriate Lord Darlington." Letting out a soft laugh, she shook her head, even though her stomach swirled with nervousness. "It would not be seemly for a lady only newly out in society to step out into the darkness with a gentleman that she was only just acquainted with."

"But would it not be exciting?" the gentleman replied, with a wiggle of his eyebrows. "Do you not think that such a thing might be a little daring? Are not all newly out young ladies known to be a little daring?"

This was something that she had never heard before and thus Cassandra shook her head, only to become all the more distressed when Lord Darlington began to lead her towards the open doors at the end of the ballroom rather than take her back to where Lady Yardley was waiting

"Lord Darlington," she protested, her voice soft instead of being loud and fierce as she had intended. "I do believe I said that I did not wish to join you."

"But I am sure I can convince you." came the reply as he grinned at her, seeming to think this was some sort of great entertainment. "I believe that once you have taken only a few steps out of doors you will –"

"Excuse me, but I must interrupt." Cassandra's heart was hammering furiously, her chest almost painful as she turned her head to see none other than Lord Sherbourne stepping up beside her. His eyes were narrowed, his forehead creased, and his eyebrows low but it was not on her his gaze was fixed, but rather on Lord Darlington. "Lord Darlington," he continued, twisting until he stood directly in front of the gentleman so that he could not make his escape. "It seems to me that you are leading Lady Cassandra *away* from where she ought to be going. Have you lost the direction of Lady Yardley?"

Carefully, Cassandra began to move her hand away from Lord's Darlington's arm only for the gentleman to reach across and clamp his hand over hers.

"No, I had not," came the sharp reply. "I thought only to lead Lady Cassandra around the room for a moment before returning her to Lady Yardley. I am sure you can understand my desire to be in her company a little longer."

No doubt this was meant as a compliment, and to make Cassandra feel rather delighted over his consideration of her, but all she felt was disdain and, recoiling from him again, she tried to pull her hand away for the second time.

"That is most understandable but also very inconsiderate of you." Lord Sherbourne lifted an eyebrow. "I am sure you are aware that there are many other dances to take place this evening. Surely you would not want any other gentleman to miss out on their dance because of your selfishness?" So saying, he inclined his head and then offered his hand to Cassandra. "Come, Lady Cassandra. Allow me to take you back to Lady Yardley, where the next gentleman will soon be waiting."

Much to Cassandra's relief, there was no other choice but for Lord Darlington to release her. His fingers coiled around hers for just a moment before, with a heavy sigh, he stepped aside until her hand fell away. Cassandra grasped Lord Sherbourne's arm very quickly indeed, as though he were the only one keeping her safe from whatever Lord Darlington had planned. Her breath tightened in her chest as she placed her hand on his arm, feeling the strength of it underneath the fabric of his coat and with that, the relief which flooded her now that he had stepped in.

"Good evening, Lord Darlington." Her soft voice drifted towards Lord Darlington as, without another word, Lord Sherbourne led her away. They had only taken a few steps before she let out a breath that she had not known she'd been holding. "I thank you so very much for taking me away from him." Slowly, her heart began to quieten its frantic pacing as Lord Sherbourne gently guided her back toward Lady Yardley. "I thought him the most amiable of gentlemen at first, and I did not expect him to do anything so... improper." Lord Sherbourne shook his head. He did not look at her but kept his gaze fixed straight ahead. The tightness of his jaw, however, betrayed his anger. "I am sorry if I behaved incorrectly."

"You did nothing wrong." Lord Sherbourne shot her a quick look. "He was attempting to take you out of doors to the gardens?" Cassandra nodded, her face burning with humiliation. "Unfortunately, he has done such things before, with other young ladies."

Her breath caught as she realized just how poor a reputation Lord Darlington must have – a reputation she had not even allowed herself to consider. She had been so caught up in the excitement of the moment, flattered and pleased at his attentions, that she had quite forgotten to even *think* what a gentleman might be hiding about himself.

"Oh..."

"Do not think that you did anything to merit this." Lord Sherbourne finally turned his head and gave her a brief smile, though his hazel eyes were now unusually dark. "Lord Darlington is well known for seeking out those in their first Season. Lady Yardley was determined to keep an eye on you, but I believe became distracted by another young lady – one of your friends - who was also in difficulty." Cassandra's gaze shifted, only to see Miss Millington standing close to Lady Yardley. Her face was white, her hands clenched tightly together in front of her, and immediately, Cassandra's heart began to race again. Whatever had happened? "Your cousin, Lady Yardley."

Lord Sherbourne nodded, gave Lady Yardley a brief smile, and then made to step away, only for Cassandra to catch his arm.

"Wait a moment, if you please." Taking a breath, she turned back to her cousin, swallowing hard. "Norah, I must inform you that Lord Sherbourne has saved my reputation this evening. I was foolish in my belief that all gentlemen are as amiable, as genteel, and as proper as I expected. Had it not been for his haste, then I am certain that Lord Darlington would have taken me from your company and out of doors, as he clearly intended."

Lady Yardley did not respond immediately other than to close her eyes. Letting out a slow breath, she then stepped forward and took Cassandra's hand, meeting her eyes.

"I am sorry that I did not see him attempting such a thing." Her soft voice spoke of frustration and perhaps, even a hint of anger. "That is my failing."

Cassandra shook her head.

"Pray, do not trouble yourself. I understand that something happened with Miss Millington?"

Her gaze went to her friend, who was standing quite still, biting her lip.

"Yes." Lady Yardley let out a long breath. "You are not the only one who has been mistreated by a gentleman this evening. She is quite safe, however." Cassandra's eyes swiveled towards her friend, and Miss Millington managed a small, yet nearly tearful smile. Cassandra did not dare ask what had happened, seeing how Miss Millington's emotions hovered far too close to the surface for her to answer such a question at this point. The last thing that her friend required was to burst into tears! "Thank you, Lord Sherbourne," Lady Yardley continued, taking a long breath and setting her shoulders. "I think perhaps that something must be done. Perhaps, Cassandra, you could ask your friends to call upon us tomorrow for afternoon tea?"

A little surprised, Cassandra found herself nodding.

"Yes, of course, Norah. I should be glad to do so. Is there any particular reason?"

"Yes, there is," came the reply. "I will teach you everything I know about society. I will tell you about the gentlemen here in London, and we will devise ways to make certain that *any* gentleman who shows even the smallest interest in you is worthy of your attention in return."

Closing her eyes briefly, Cassandra found herself struggling against sharp tears. In only one single evening, her dreams and hopes of what society would be like, and of how the gentlemen would behave, had been shattered. Her cousin had tried to warn her, and she had not fully accepted what had been said. Now, however, there was no choice but for her to do so. With a deep breath and a lift her chin, Cassandra opened her eyes and tried to smile at her cousin.

"Thank you, cousin Norah. I do think that sounds like a good idea, for we all need to hear what you have to say." Her shoulders slumped a little. "I, it seems, most of all."

CHAPTER FIVE

"*G*ood afternoon."

Jonathan walked into Lord Yardley's drawing room, to be greeted by Lady Yardley and Lady Cassandra. There was no smile on either of their faces, however and, given the serious feel of the room, Jonathan felt as though he had walked into a somewhat serious situation. Whatever was the matter?

"Thank you for attending." Lady Yardley smiled at him but it faded rather quickly. "I hope you are aware that Lord Yardley has returned to his estate?"

"Yes, I did know."

"And, therefore, I believe we may need your help."

"My help?" A little surprised, Jonathan spread his hands. "I do not know what exactly it is I can do to help you." An idea came to him and he sucked in a breath. "If this is about last evening and Lord Darlington, I can only apologize for not stepping in more quickly."

"No, it is not about Lord Darlington." It was Lady Cassandra who spoke, rising from her chair and coming towards him. To his utter astonishment, she settled one hand on his arm, her eyes soft as she looked into his. "I am so very grateful to you for what you did. I dread to think what would have happened had Lord Darlington managed to drag me out of doors."

Her frame was shaken by a slight shudder, her fingers wrapping a little more tightly around his arm, and Jonathan found himself eager to comfort her, putting his free hand on top of hers.

"I am certain that you would have found a way out of it." Taking a breath, he shook his head. "Lord Darlington is not a good sort. He is something of a rogue, in fact, inclined to prey on young ladies who are new to society."

"Which is where I think we may need your help." Lady Yardley began, as Lady Cassandra dropped her hand from Jonathan's arm, turning back to her cousin. "I have told Lady Cassandra and her friends that I will assist them in their efforts to each find a suitable gentleman for themself. In addition, I have also suggested gently that you may be willing to aid us there."

Jonathan blinked.

"Truly?"

Lady Yardley chuckled.

"Yes, though you need not appear so shocked! You are a good gentleman with an excellent character, and both my husband and I think you an exceptional fellow."

A little uncertain as to what it was Lady Yardley was asking of him, Jonathan determined not to agree to anything straight away.

"I believe you will have to explain it to me a little more before I say anything further."

Before Lady Yardley could explain, however, Lady Cassandra spoke up.

"My cousin is attempting to help both myself and my

friends in seeking out suitable gentlemen," she began, her face a little pink although her gaze was steady. "I am well aware that you may see that there are many excellent fellows in London, but what you may not realize is that my friends and I have determined that we will not marry a gentleman simply for the sake of it. There must be an affection there, at the very least! There must be the beginnings of love. None of us will marry a gentleman simply because he is handsome, or because he has a great deal of wealth, or because he carries a suitable title. That is the very *last* thing we wish for."

Jonathan stared at Lady Cassandra for some moments, resisting the urge to let a bubble of harsh laughter rise up within him. He wanted to tell her not to hope for such a thing, wanted to state that most gentlemen did not care for the idea of a love match, but the moment he opened his mouth, his heart twisted. Rather than holding her penetrating gaze, he dropped his to the floor.

"I am afraid, my dear, that Lord Sherbourne does not believe in such a thing as a love match."

Lady Yardley smiled softly, her eyes rather heavy, as though she felt sorry for him in his lack of belief.

"That is not *exactly* true," Jonathan protested, finding the wide-eyed look of Lady Cassandra to be a little too much to bear. "I am sure that such things can take place, but would say that they can be a little... rare." Seeing Lady Yardley's eyebrows lift, he cleared his throat, warmth flooding upwards. "Though, of course, you would say such a thing about your own match to Lord Yardley, calling it a love match, would you not?"

Lady Yardley chuckled at his attempt to defend himself.

"Yes, indeed, I would. But this is not about myself and

Lord Yardley, this is about you, and your beliefs as regards love."

Jonathan blinked, his throat constricting. How had he come from talking about how he could aid Lady Cassandra to this? He had no urge to talk about his thoughts on matters of the heart, particularly not with a young lady who seemed to draw herself *into* his heart, no matter what he tried!

"Yes, Lord Sherbourne." Lady Cassandra began to move towards him, her steps slow, her eyes a little wide still. "I should very much like to know what your position is on such things. When it comes time for you to wed, will you seek out a love match or –"

"Certainly, I will not." the words came out of his mouth before he could stop them, aware of how sharply her eyebrows lifted. "I am afraid that I am very practically minded, Lady Cassandra. That is not to say that I will not support you and your idea, however, but for myself, I am entirely of the opposite view." This conversation was quickly becoming mortifying, for his face began to burn as Lady Cassandra shook her head, sighed and turned away from him. For whatever reason, it seemed as though she was disappointed in him, and her response in turning away made his heart twist in his chest. He opened his mouth, his heart wanting him to say more, perhaps even to defend himself but, after a moment, he simply shrugged both shoulders and held his hands behind his back. Reminding himself silently that he did not need to defend his position to anyone, he nodded in Lady Yardley's direction. "Please explain exactly what it is you wish me to do, if you would."

Lady Yardley sat down, gesturing to a chair and waiting for him to take a seat as Lady Cassandra sat down too.

"Lady Cassandra's friends will be here within the hour. I should like to suggest to them that I will find a way to make certain that the gentlemen they consider – or who seem to be considering them – are exactly who they appear to be. You know as well as I that oftentimes, gentlemen can hide their true selves, although, of course, ladies may also do so. Therefore, I wish very much to make sure that not only my cousin but also her friends, are given the opportunity to find a suitable match with a gentleman who is honest about himself and his character, so that they might give him their heart without any concern."

Nodding Slowly, Jonathan began to understand what Lady Yardley meant.

"And you wish me to aid you in some way?"

She nodded.

"There will be times when I will miss something," wincing, she gestured towards Lady Cassandra, "just as I did last evening. The truth is, I did not know about Lord Darlington's reputation, but *you* did. Perhaps you would be willing to assist my niece, for example, in being aware of which gentlemen might truly wish her company, and which are paying their attentions to her only for their own gain. I would ask my husband but, given that he has gone back to the estate, there is no one else to turn to."

"I would be so very grateful." Lady Cassandra spread out both hands. "There are so very many gentlemen, and I think the three who gave me specific compliments last evening do not have any goodness in their character, even though I initially believed them to be genuine."

Frowning, Jonathan tilted his head.

"Dare I ask which gentlemen they were?"

Lady Cassandra hesitated, but then gave him the names of two others aside from Lord Darlington. Jonathan could only nod, not wanting her to think that he was criticizing her in any way for accepting their compliments, but inwardly realizing just how much Lady Cassandra needed assistance.

"I am sure that you will tell me that none of those gentlemen truly sought my company and that none of them had any real interest in furthering their acquaintance with me."

The hopelessness in Lady Cassandra's voice had Jonathan's heart burning with sympathy, but he forced himself to be honest.

"I am afraid it is so, but that is not to say it is your fault. It is something that every young lady who comes to London must learn." Sighing heavily, Lady Cassandra closed her eyes.

"If you would be willing to help guide both me and my friends, Lord Sherbourne – despite your disbelief in love matches being a wise choice – then I would be so very grateful."

The weight in her expression and the sadness in her voice had his heart leaping toward her and he found himself nodding before he had truly made a decision.

"Yes, of course. Whatever I can do to be of assistance to you."

In an instant, the heaviness was gone from her features as she smiled at him... only for her eyes to flare and her smile to fade a little.

"But we will not be keeping you from your own attempts at finding a match, I hope?"

At this, Lady Yardley began to laugh but rather than join in with her, a frown crossed Jonathan's forehead.

"You need not worry about Lord Sherbourne, my dear." Lady Yardley remarked, either not seeing or ignoring his frown. "He is not interested in considering matrimony as yet. Is that not so?"

Jonathan wanted to tell her that yes, in fact, he *was* considering matrimony and that yes, he would be seeking out a bride for himself simply to chase away the laughter, but his untruths could not be brought to the fore. He had just finished arguing with his mother over whether or not he was soon to bring a bride back to his estate, and could not speak falsehoods now.

"Is that so, Lord Sherbourne?"

Lady Cassandra's quiet question seemed to stab at his heart and he looked away. For some reason, he could not seem to look into her eyes, and yet she seemed determined to gaze into his.

"That is so." His jaw felt tight, the words burning, struggling to escape from him, but he spoke them, nonetheless. "I have no intention of matrimony this Season."

"Oh, how wonderful!"

Much to his surprise, Lady Cassandra smiled warmly at him. A surge of hope raced through his veins, as, for a moment, he thought that she was about to say how relieved she was, in the hope that they might begin a closer acquaintance. Of *course*, that was not what she had been planning to say! Such a thought was a very strange one, and Jonathan threw it aside, just as Lady Cassandra expressed how grateful she was to know that his assistance would not bring him any particular difficulty of his own. Of course, she would not express a desire to draw closer to him! That was foolishness indeed and why he had ever thought of such a thing, he did not know.

"I am very grateful to you." Lady Yardley smiled gently. "I will call for some refreshments, for the other young ladies will be here very soon, and should you wish to stay, you are most welcome. Otherwise, you and I can speak again very soon."

Finding that he was greatly confused by his current feelings towards Lady Cassandra and the hope which had surged through him, Jonathan quickly got to his feet.

"I shall speak to you again at another time." He gave Lady Yardley a quick bow, flicked another glance towards Lady Cassandra, and then hurried from the room. It was only when he had stepped into the hallway, however, that somebody called his name. Turning his head, he discovered that Lady Cassandra had come out of the drawing room and was hurrying towards him. There were two footmen in the hallway, both standing ahead of him but, all the same, Jonathan found his heart quickening a little. He did not want to be in any way improper, but being practically alone with Lady Cassandra, albeit for only a few moments, was a little thrilling. "Lady Cassandra?"

She smiled as she reached him, her blue eyes searching his expression.

"I wanted to tell you again just how grateful I am for what you did last evening. I know just how careful one must be with one's reputation. I know that it can be gone in a moment. And I am all too aware that last night might have been that moment, had it not been for you."

Jonathan shook his head.

"You need not continually express your thanks." He shrugged and placed both hands behind his back, fearful that he might reach to hold her hand, or some other foolishness, should they linger in conversation any longer. Lady Cassandra's smile remained and she made no attempt to hurry back to the drawing room. Instead, she simply held his gaze for a few moments and then with small sigh, bit the edge of her lip. Jonathan tilted his head a little. "Is there something more you wish to say?"

Lady Cassandra let out a slightly nervous laugh but nodded.

"I have no doubt you will think me quite ridiculous, but I promised Lord Darlington my first waltz whenever I am permitted to dance it." She nibbled the edge of her lip again, her eyes going to the floor, her cheeks flushing. "No doubt it was foolishness to say such a thing to him, but now I feel as though I am obliged."

"You have not been given permission to dance the waltz as yet, however."

"I have been granted it. Lord Yardley told me so before he took his leave." Lady Cassandra spread out both hands. "If I promised it to Lord Darlington, am I permitted to take it from him again?" Her hands dropped to her sides. "Or would that be very bad form?"

Chuckling, Jonathan shrugged lightly, his hands falling to his sides, despite his previous resolve to keep them safely behind his back.

"It may be a *little* of bad form, Lady Cassandra, but it is understandable. If you like, I shall stand up with you for your first waltz, rather than worrying about Lord Darlington coming to seek it from you."

Lady Cassandra's eyes widened, and her breath caught in a gasp as she stared at him, clearly a little taken aback by what he had offered her. The next moment she had stepped forward and, putting both of her hands to his, grasped his fingers tightly.

"You truly are a very gracious gentleman." Her voice was a little wispy, as though it was a struggle to get the words out. "Thank you very much, Lord Sherbourne. I do not have to worry about my first waltz now."

Jonathan tried to smile, but his mouth seemed frozen in place.

"Mayhap you will be able to look forward to it now, rather than be concerned about it."

"I believe that I shall." Standing on tiptoe, Lady Cassandra pressed a light kiss to his cheek and then with a quiet giggle, turned away. "Thank you again, Lord Sherbourne."

Waiting until Lady Cassandra had turned into the drawing room, Jonathan let out his breath in a slow hiss. The imprint of her lips on his cheek burned, and he only then realized just how quickly his heart was beating. He had never responded to any young lady in a manner such as this. It had only been a kiss on his cheek, so why now was he so overcome by it? She was not the first young lady who had done such a thing... but she certainly was the first young lady to whom he had responded so strongly.

Jonathan gave himself a shake before turning to stride down the hallway, one hand pressed to his cheek. Whatever was happening to him, it was entirely to do with Lady Cassandra. The fact that he had now agreed to help her in securing a suitable gentleman - a gentleman who would fall in love with her, seemed a good deal more foolish than he had ever thought it might be. What he ought to do, Jonathan considered, was stay as far away from her as possible.

Except now, it was much too late.

CHAPTER SIX

"Thank you to all for attending."

Miss Wynch shot Cassandra a broad smile before she spoke, directing her words to Lady Yardley.

"We are all very grateful to you," she responded as the other young ladies nodded. "You are very kind to offer to help us."

Lady Yardley smiled.

"I am glad to be able to." Her smile continued to grow as she spread her hands. "I myself was someone who found the very same desire within myself as all of you do at present: the desire for a suitable match with a loving gentleman."

"And you were able to find one."

In answer to Lady Almeria's statement, Lady Yardley nodded.

"I was, although it was not without difficulty." She tilted her head, smiled again, and then gestured to all of them. "Which is why I now seek to help you. If I can share with you some of my wisdom... and some of my tricks to aid you in finding a suitable fellow then I shall."

It was this last remark which had Cassandra sitting up a little straighter.

"Tricks?" she repeated as her cousin laughed softly "Whatever do you mean?"

She glanced at her friends, seeing how each of them now paid a little more attention, their gazes fixed on Lady Yardley and every head turned towards her. They had only ever had instruction on how to behave correctly, how to talk, how to dress, and how to respond appropriately to any situation – so to hear the mention of trickery was, to Cassandra's mind, both interesting and also a little disconcerting

"Since you are new to society, you may not have heard of a small publication that comes out on a fortnightly basis," Lady Yardley began. "I have indulged in the ownership of it for some years. It is by no means a secret that my name is attached to it, however, although I often have others writing for me. I do not claim to write every piece myself."

Cassandra blinked rapidly. There were some society papers, and certainly the newspapers, which her father and brother had always sought out, but what Lady Yardley could be involved in, Cassandra could not imagine! Such things were not expected of a lady of quality but, then again, Cassandra considered, why should a lady such as Lady Yardley *not* do such a thing? There was nothing wrong with it in itself and given that it was no secret that she wrote such things, then there could be nothing for anyone to complain about.

"What is the name of the publication, if you do not mind my asking?"

It was Lady Elizabeth who asked the question, her eyes as wide as Cassandra knew her own to be.

"It is 'The London Ledger'."

The name meant very little to Cassandra herself, but

given the way her friends exclaimed, it appeared that she was the only one who had very little knowledge of it

"But that is astonishing!" another one of her friends exclaimed "It is a very well-known publication, though my mother has never allowed me to read it."

Surprise filled Cassandra, immediately beginning to wonder what sort of things were being printed in 'The London Ledger' which would prevent a young lady from being permitted to read it!

"There is nothing improper written there," Lady Yardley began, as though she could read Cassandra's thoughts." Lady Yardley took a sip of her tea, as though discussing this was quite commonplace "I have many others who write for me, as I have said – both ladies and gentlemen, in fact. I always seek to print what is true. However, I will admit that, on occasion, I have been forced to print a rumor with the caveat that it is *always* explained to be so." So saying, she set her teacup down on the table beside her. "There have always been good reasons for such things. I never print whispers lightly."

Considering this for a moment, Cassandra shook her head.

"I am afraid that I do not understand." The confusion in her voice brought a quietness to the rest of the room as Cassandra let her gaze run around her friends, looking from one to the next, and then, finally, to her cousin "Why should you ever need to print a rumor?"

"I understand your concern." Lady Yardley replied, quietly. "No doubt, you have always been told that rumors are to be avoided at all costs."

"Yes, precisely." Cassandra let out a long breath. "My mother states that rumors are nothing short of gossip. Therefore, I determined never to even *listen* to them."

"As did I," Miss Wynch added as some of the other young ladies nodded. "I can understand Lady Cassandra's confusion."

"I shall explain." Smiling gently and without any hint of frustration over their questions, Lady Yardley lifted one shoulder. "Every time I have printed a rumor – explaining it to be so, of course, it has been, I considered, in the best interests of the *ton*. For example, the last time I did so, it was to protect a young lady – much like yourselves. She was being courted by a worthy gentleman but, in the midst of this, some rumors were circulating – rumors my husband heard. I shall not go into details but they were very dark whispers indeed." Her expression grew serious. "I could not prove whether or not such whispers were true, but I could instead make certain that the young lady, whom he was eager to attach himself to, knew of them also."

A frown swept across Cassandra's forehead.

"Could you not simply have spoken to the young lady in question?"

Lady Yardley sighed.

"I had tried, but the young lady, who felt she was so close to being betrothed, was a little less than willing to hear anything I had to say. She would not listen to anything about her particular gentleman. To be truthful, I also attempted to speak with her mother in the hope that my concerns would overrule the delight of having a daughter so close to being betrothed. However, my concern was not taken seriously – and thus, I felt I had no choice."

"And did they listen?"

Lady Yardley smiled sadly.

"For some reason, printing words in a paper gave my concerns more weight and yes, the courtship came to an end soon afterward. I therefore felt justified in what I had done."

A brief silence filled the room as the tightness in Cassandra's stomach began to unwind.

"And have you ever been proven wrong?"

This time it was Miss Millington who spoke up, her hands clasped together, her fingers loosening and tightening, and her eyes a little wide. Did she have some sympathy for the situation which Lady Yardley had only just described?

"There was one occasion where the rumors were not proven to be true." Lady Yardley smiled again, her expression almost a satisfied one. "But in that situation, the gentleman was forced to prove himself to his lady, which made for a very satisfactory outcome. They are very happily married now, and have, indeed, found a love match with each other - which is all the more wonderful." She let out another small sigh. "As I have said. I am always very careful about what I print, but it is an excellent way of making sure that certain gentlemen who are eager to prove themselves to their chosen lady are, in fact, genuine in their affections."

Cassandra considered this for some moments. Did Norah intend to use 'The London Ledger' to aid each of them? It could be of use, she imagined.

"What are your intentions with 'The London Ledger' as regards us?" Choosing not to hold back her questions, she looked at her cousin steadily. "You will use it to help us, I assume?"

"I should hope so. In the first instance, myself and Lord Sherbourne – a friend of both myself and my husband – will be able to advise you on whether or not the gentleman pursuing you might have anything of concern about him. If there are rumors or whispers of some kind, then the Ledger can be used to discover the truth. If there are none, however, then I would suggest that you may have found a gentleman willing to commit his heart to you, in time, should your acquaintance progress that far."

A gentle swirl of excitement began to rise within Cassandra as she quickly imagined what it would be like to find herself betrothed – only for it to fade away as she thought about what it would be like to be betrothed to a gentleman who did not have any real interest in her and had only proposed to her for the satisfaction of his pleasures or requirements. She knew all too well that her dowry was a significant one, albeit smaller than her elder sister's – but more than enough to make a gentleman wish to claim her as his own. The more she thought about it, the more she realized just how much help she needed in finding what she wanted the most: a gentleman who would love her.

"I think then, that I would be glad to accept, Lady Yardley," Lady Elizabeth stated, as the others murmured their agreement also. "And with Lord Sherbourne helping us, I am sure that we will find ourselves in the very best of situations."

"I am looking forward to Lord Sherbourne's company." Miss Millington's eyes glowed with a sudden fire. "You say that he is to be of aid to us also, Lady Yardley? That is very good of him."

As Lady Yardley launched an explanation about how Lord Sherbourne had often helped her and Lord Yardley in her writing of 'The London Ledger', Cassandra battled with a sense of jealousy. Jealousy that she had not in the least bit expected, but was present, nonetheless. Why ever should she be jealous over Miss Millington's obvious delight in the fact Lord Sherbourne would be assisting them? He certainly was a handsome fellow with his dark hair, square jaw, and swirling hazel eyes, but that did not mean that there was any particular interest on Cassandra's part... or was there?

Biting the edge of her lip, Cassandra's frown drew across her forehead as she looked away from her friend, recalling how Lord Sherbourne had assisted her the previous evening. How grateful she had been to him for coming to rescue her from Lord Darlington and his less than proper schemes! She had been grateful for his strength, his determination, and his willingness to break into a conversation and take her away from the gentleman without even a flicker of hesitation. When she had kissed his cheek earlier that afternoon, the gentle warmth of his skin on hers had made her heart leap, but she had put it down to a mere sense of gratitude rather than anything else. Surely it could not be that she was drawn to the very gentleman who, only a short time ago, had declared himself entirely unwilling to wed! No, that would be nothing but foolishness, and she would not allow herself to be foolish.

"What say you, Cassandra?"

Turning her attention back to her cousin, Cassandra took in Lady Yardley's smile.

"I think it is an excellent idea," she declared, smiling at her cousin. "After yesterday evening, where I was almost stolen away by a gentleman whom I considered to be amiable, I am more aware of my need for as much help as I can get!" Her smile slipped a little. "Society is not as I thought it would be, and I believe that my ideas about quickly finding a handsome, loving gentleman to call my own were entirely foolish. I see now that not every gentleman is as he appears, which does leave me with the question as to how I am to discover the truth about their character!"

"And that is where both I and Lord Sherbourne step in," her cousin reassured her. "We will find you an excellent fellow by the end of the Season, I am sure." She gestured to the entire room. "No matter how many Seasons it takes, I shall be here to help all of you."

"And we shall be here for each other too," Cassandra added as her friends nodded. "We have all made a promise to aid one another in our search for a gentleman who will love and care for us. Whether I find a husband this Season or next, I shall come to London every year until *all* of us are wed, settled and happy. I promise it."

"As do I."

Lady Elizabeth smiled at her and, as the rest of her friends pledged this also, Cassandra pressed one hand to her heart, aware of tears prickling in her eyes and the happy smile on her lips. Last evening had brought into sharp relief just how little she knew of society, but now she felt a good deal more confident. She was protected, surrounded by those who cared for her – and she for them. She had nothing to worry herself about unduly any longer. With her cousin, Lord Sherbourne, and 'The London Ledger', she would be able to find out the truth about any gentleman's character before she gave her heart to him, and that seemed to be the very best of situations.

"How do we begin?" she asked, now a good deal more eager than before.

"Well." Lady Yardley laughed as Cassandra smiled at her. "You go back into town, back into society, and enjoy as many balls, soirees, and afternoon teas as you please. But should a gentleman step forward and begin to make his attentions known to you, then I suggest that you come and speak with us about him, so we may find out as much as we can of him. If you desire to return such attentions, and the gentleman in question appears eager to further his connection with you, then, should he be just as he seems, all shall be well. But if you find no particular interest in him, then I would encourage you to treat him accordingly – not cruelly, but without any obvious interest in returning his attentions. There is no shame in behaving so, for I assure you, you will not find love with a gentleman in whom you have no interest."

Cassandra nodded slowly, those words resonating within her. Her mother and father had never shown any particular interest in the sort of gentleman whom Cassandra might wish to marry, but in the little they had said, there had never been any mention of love. The only advice which had been given to her was that, if a gentleman was favorably titled, well-connected, wealthy, and willing to marry her, Cassandra should accept without hesitation. There was never any thought of affection or interest and thus, it was something of a relief to hear her cousin speak so very differently and with such determination.

"Perhaps we should also tell each other which gentlemen we ought to stay away from." A wry smile tipped the edge of her mouth. "Lord Darlington would be one such gentleman, I am afraid."

"Certainly, he should be!" Her cousin agreed as the other young ladies shared a look. "I believe you also have a gentleman you would wish to place on that list, Miss Millington?"

Miss Millington nodded but, much to Cassandra's concern, she shuddered lightly.

"I should like to add Lord Holdridge to that list." Her voice was soft. "In my foolishness, I thought him to be enamored of me."

Immediately, Cassandra shook her head.

"You are not foolish, my dear friend."

"I was." Miss Millington managed a smile as she took in a deep breath. "But I shall never be so again."

Lady Yardley also smiled, reaching across to squeeze Miss Millington's hand for a moment.

"I assure you, if we do as we have planned, no unscrupulous gentlemen will be able to take advantage of any of you. You will see a gentleman's heart and whether or not it is open to love – and, I promise you that, in due course, you will all find your hope of happiness fulfilled. It may take a little time, but love is coming."

Cassandra smiled, pressing one hand to her heart. *And my heart is ready to receive it.*

CHAPTER SEVEN

"Good evening, Lady Cassandra."

Jonathan's eyes had found the lady the very moment that she stepped into the room. He had not meant to do it, but it was as though something within him had drawn itself to her. Reminding himself that he was meant to be helping the young lady, rather than finding himself drawn to her, he nonetheless offered his arm.

"Good evening, Lord Sherbourne."

"Should you like a turn about the room?"

Lady Cassandra glanced back towards Lady Yardley who was only a step or two behind them. She nodded with a smile and Lady Cassandra quickly gave her acceptance.

"Come then." His heart lifted a little as she fell into step beside him. "I hear that you and your friends have had your discussion with Lady Yardley. Do you feel a little more confident, now, to traverse the rocky ground that is London society?"

Lady Cassandra laughed, a blush coloring her cheeks prettily.

"Yes, we had an excellent conversation and yes, I feel a

good deal better. I will admit to you that I felt rather foolish in how unguarded I was, particularly when it came to Lord Darlington. That foolishness will not remain within me, however, and thus I am sure that this evening will be a most enjoyable one."

"I believe you are right." Jonathan smiled, aware of just how quickly his heart was beating in his chest. "I did not think that Lady Yardley would tell you about 'The London Ledger', though I am glad that she has. It is not a secret, of course, but neither is it something she speaks about very often. It is a wise thought to use it for the benefit of you and your friends."

"I believe that everything my cousin does is done with wisdom." A gentle sigh came from her as she turned her head away. "Would that *I* had such wisdom."

Finding himself eager to reassure her, Jonathan pressed her hand for a moment, then withdrew.

"You will find that such wisdom comes with simply being a part of society, particularly here in London." Wincing slightly, he shook his head. "It does not mean that everyone within it is malicious, nor that every gentleman is a rogue, only to say that it is wise to be able to distinguish one from the other. It is good that Lady Yardley seeks to help you there, for many a young lady finds herself a little overwhelmed!"

"And you are here to guide me also." The warmth of her tone made Jonathan's heart leap all the more. "I am very grateful to you."

Jonathan wanted to tell her that he was rather glad to be able to do this for her, that he enjoyed spending time with her, but the words did not come. Instead, he simply walked around the ballroom with her, taking everything in and being all too aware of just how his heart was affected by being so close to her. The feelings which had come to the fore when she had first walked into the room at Lady Yardley's residence when he had first set eyes on Lady Cassandra, had not disappeared as he had believed they would. Instead, they lingered, growing slowly and wrapping themselves all the more around his heart. Jonathan told himself that it was foolishness to be drawn to the lady but, regardless of what he wanted, his growing affection seemed determined to make itself a home within his heart. Walking with her in such a manner as this was probably not a good idea, given that it would only increase such feelings, but what could be done now? He had promised that he would be of aid to Lady Cassandra and her friends, so he could not step back from her now! Reminding himself that he had no intention of marrying, nor even courting *any* young lady of his acquaintance, Jonathan cleared his throat and looked around the room once more.

"There are many fine gentlemen here this evening. I am sure that once I have released you, you will have a great many fellows coming to seek you out in the hope of dancing with you."

"Do you think so?"

The slight wobble in her voice betrayed her concern.

"Certainly, I do – though I should advise you not to dance with Lord Darlington." Jonathan laughed as Lady Cassandra smiled up at him. "To be serious, it is perfectly suitable for you to dance with any gentleman who asks. Unless, of course, he is well known to be a rogue or a scoundrel, in which case you may refuse him."

Lady Cassandra stopped suddenly, turning to face him, her eyes wide.

"But how am I to know which gentlemen are rogues and scoundrels? I knew there would be one or two such gentlemen, but I believe now that there are a good many more than I had ever expected. How can I tell which gentlemen are of good character and which ones are not?"

Jonathan smiled, lowering his head a little.

"I shall stay nearby if you wish."

Lady Cassandra blinked for a moment, looking up at him, her hand slipping from his arm as though she could not quite believe that he had offered her such a thing.

"Do you not have any intention of dancing this evening? I am aware that you promised to help us, but surely that does not mean that you have to give up your own pleasures for our sake."

"I do not have any interest in dancing," Jonathan replied truthfully. "I have spent a few Seasons in London already, and have done a great deal of dancing, whereas you have done very little. I would be very glad indeed to make certain of your happiness this evening."

"Then you are a very kind gentleman." Lady Cassandra took his arm again, a soft sigh of contentment slipping from her lips. "Already I feel a good deal more confident."

Jonathan smiled to himself, a little surprised at the sense of satisfaction which came with being beside her. The truth was, he would usually have preferred to do as he pleased on an occasion like this. He might decide to dance, or go to play cards, or perhaps simply converse with as many of his acquaintances as he wished. But he now appeared quite content to allow Lady Cassandra to dictate what he would do with the rest of his evening. Was he truly as enamored of her as that?

"Now, listen for a moment," he murmured, leaning a little closer to her ear and choosing to put such questions aside. "Here comes Lord Ramsworth. He is an exceptionally conversational gentleman. I am sure that he would be very pleased to have your company. You should not hesitate to give it to him, only be aware that you will have very little opportunity to say anything at all!"

He chuckled as Lady Cassandra shot him a sharp look, seeking to know if he was entirely serious, only for her eyes to twinkle when she realized that he was. Lord Ramsworth was a very amiable fellow. He had never shown any desire to wed, much as Jonathan himself had not, but that did not stop him from dancing - and speaking - with as many young ladies as he could. Upon discovering anyone who was not acquainted with him, Lord Ramsworth would determine to acquaint himself with them just as soon as he was able. Lady Cassandra's mouth opened as though to say something, but Jonathan merely straightened, seeing that there was no time to say anything more, for Lord Ramsworth was now upon them.

"Good evening, Lord Sherbourne."

Jonathan inclined his head, wasting no time.

"Good evening, Lord Ramsworth. Might I introduce my new acquaintance to you?"

Lord Ramsworth's round face lit up as he grinned down at Lady Cassandra. Clearly, this was precisely what he had been hoping for

"Yes, I should be very glad indeed if you would."

Quick to oblige him, Jonathan made the introductions, and then took a small step back, allowing the gentleman to speak openly with Lady Cassandra without being interrupted. The gentleman first enquired as to whether she was enjoying the Season, asked questions about her presentation to the Queen and, eventually and almost as an afterthought, for her dance card. Jonathan chuckled quietly, only for his arm to be caught by someone to his left. Swiveling his head around, he grinned as Lord Knoxbridge nodded his head toward Lady Cassandra.

"I have not seen *her* before." His eyes lingered for a moment, and Jonathan's grin began to fade. "She is indeed a very pretty little thing."

"And the cousin of Lady Yardley." Jonathan responded quickly. "Lady Yardley is guiding her through this Season and I have agreed to assist wherever I can."

This was stated with a very pointed look in Lord Knoxbridge's direction and, on seeing it, Lord Knoxbridge let out a heavy sigh.

"And thus, you are tempted to claim her for yourself, then?"

The strange urge to state that, yes, he *was* courting Lady Cassandra, and intended to make her his own suddenly pushed itself to the forefront of Jonathan's mind. He did not say such a thing, however, shrugging and shaking his head instead of speaking a single word. Inwardly, however, he fought the idea. Why ever would he think of Lady Cassandra in that way? Yes, he had been affected when he had first laid eyes on her, but that had only been because of her beauty, had it not? Thus far she did appear to be very amiable and of a kind character... but she wanted a love match, and Jonathan himself had always rejected such an idea.

"It is a pity." Lord Knoxbridge shook his head. "I should very much have liked to dance with her... holding her close in the waltz, mayhap?"

He chuckled, but a flash of anger ran through Jonathan as he clenched his jaw tight. It was only then Lord Knoxbridge's eyes sharpened on his that Jonathan slowly released the tension now flooding through him, closing his eyes for a moment.

"Good gracious, you are taking your promise of help rather seriously, are you not?"

A wry smile ran across Jonathan's lips.

"It seems as though I am." He lifted one eyebrow. "And that means you are *not* to dance with her. In fact, I will not even introduce you to her, not when you have such dark intentions!"

"They're not dark intentions." Lord Knoxbridge waved a hand. "Even though I have enjoyed close acquaintances with one or two ladies these last few Seasons, I swear to you I shall not consider Lady Cassandra in that manner." He shrugged his shoulders. "You know that I tend to stay away from those innocents who have only just come out into society."

His anger fading to relief, Jonathan found himself nodding.

"I am pleased to hear you say such a thing." Jonathan's reply came quickly as he reconsidered his own response in light of how Lord Knoxbridge had spoken. "Very well, I will introduce you to her, but any indication of even the smallest impropriety will not be tolerated. She is to be treated with great respect."

His friend gazed back steadily into Jonathan's eyes but after a few moments of silence, agreed.

"Very well. I do admit that I find the idea of merely dancing with no further agenda to be very dull indeed."

Jonathan permitted himself a wry smile.

"It is unlike you, I know, but you must do this." Keeping his voice and gaze low, Jonathan waited until his friend had nodded once more in confirmation. Looking back to Lady Cassandra, his heart lifted into his throat as he saw that she was speaking to none other than Lord Darlington. Wherever had he appeared from? And why had Jonathan not even noticed? "Excuse me, Knoxbridge."

Moving quickly, he came to stand by Lady Cassandra's side, only for Lord Knoxbridge to come to stand beside him. Throwing a glance at Lady Cassandra, Jonathan caught the smile on her lips, but not in her eyes. All in all, she appeared a little fraught, for her eyes were not lit with light nor her expression gentle. Her hands were not held loosely by her sides, but clasped tightly together in front of her. All in all, she looked distinctly uncomfortable.

"Lord Darlington," the young lady continued, gesturing quickly to Jonathan himself. "Whilst I may be permitted now to dance the waltz, I fear I already have Lord Sherbourne's name there on my dance card."

"That is most unfair!" Lord Darlington threw up his hands. "Sherbourne, you must step aside, I am promised to the young lady."

Reaching out for her dance card he made to tug it from her wrist, but Jonathan took a step forward and Lord Darlington immediately pulled his hand back to his side.

"I am afraid the matter is settled, Darlington." Keeping both hands behind his back, Jonathan held his gaze towards Lord Darlington. "It is the lady's prerogative as to who she gives her first waltz to, and if it is not to you, then such a circumstance is something you simply must accept."

"That is not what was promised." Lord Darlington scowled, stamping his foot once on the floor as his eyes roved from Jonathan to Lady Cassandra and back again. "I am most displeased."

Jonathan rolled his eyes.

"It is a lady's prerogative," he stated again.

Glancing at Lord Knoxbridge, he widened his eyes in an attempt to encourage his friend to agree with him, and he let out a breath of relief when Lord Knoxbridge understood at once.

"I quite agree. If she has promised the waltz to another, then it is gone from you, Darlington." Lord Knoxbridge shrugged. "You cannot complain about that. Surely there are many other young ladies you could dance with in Lady Cassandra's place?"

Lord Darlington only scowled. He did not give a single word in answer but instead turned on his heel and marched away across the room, as if to state that, if he could not dance with Lady Cassandra, he would dance with no one else.

Lady Cassandra let out a long breath and closed her eyes, one hand on his arm, as she steadied herself.

"Thank you, Lord Sherbourne. Again, I am in your debt."

"No, it was my fault. I promised you that I should be here to make certain that Lord Darlington could not take the waltz from you, and then I found myself distracted." Gesturing to Lord Knoxbridge, he threw his friend a smile. "Although I appreciate your support, Knoxbridge, enough to forgive you the distraction."

"As do I."

Lady Cassandra dipped into a brief curtsey, a gentle flush again rising in her cheeks, making her all the more beautiful to Jonathan's mind.

"And that, it seems, is Lord Sherbourne's terrible way of making an introduction." Lord Knoxbridge laughed, shook his head, and bowed. "Good evening, Lady Cassandra. I am very glad to make your acquaintance. Lord Sherbourne speaks very highly of you."

Lady Cassandra's eyes widened, but Jonathan only

shrugged, refusing to give any explanation of what he had said of her.

"And since I am not to have the waltz, might I be offered your dance card so that I can take another for myself?" Lord Knoxbridge continued, stealing away Lady Cassandra's attention again. "I should be delighted to stand up with you."

Lady Cassandra smiled, dropped her gaze, mumbled something, and handed it to him.

"I still have a good many dances remaining, Lord Knoxbridge." Appearing a little embarrassed, Lady Cassandra licked her lips, her head tilting forward. "I had wished to have had a few more filled. I do hope that I will only have a few dances to step back from, for I do so very much enjoy dancing."

"But you are to take only the *one* dance," Jonathan warned, elbowing his friend as Lady Cassandra looked from him to the other and back again, her eyes a little wide. "Yes, Lady Cassandra. Lord Knoxbridge is one such gentleman who is not to be trusted."

This was said with a grin and though Lord Knoxbridge rolled his eyes, he ultimately could not help but agree.

"Indeed, Lady Cassandra, I shall return you immediately to Lord Sherbourne's side the moment the dance is at an end."

"I am glad to hear it," Jonathan replied, sending a wink in Lady Cassandra's direction. She caught it, her smile lifting as she looked at him from under her lashes. At that moment, Jonathan's grin fixed itself to his face, his heart clattering against his chest, and he could not even recall what they had been talking of. It was not until his friend nudged him that he finally caught himself again, clearing his throat and tugging his gaze away.

"The cotillion is upon us!" Lord Knoxbridge grinned as he offered Lady Cassandra his arm. "Do not fear, Lord Sherbourne. I shall have the lady back soon enough."

Jonathan tried to laugh, but the sound knotted in his throat. Why he should find himself so spellbound by the young lady was quite inexplicable. He had met many beautiful young ladies in the last few Seasons but none had come to capture him in the way that Lady Cassandra had. He had never felt such emotions before. It was so very confusing, and he did not know whether he wanted to embrace it or run from it.

One thing was certain, however: he was now looking forward to the waltz with a good deal more enthusiasm. He could hardly wait for the moment when he could take Lady Cassandra into his arms and experience what it would be like to hold her so close.

That time was only a few minutes away.

CHAPTER EIGHT

"*A*nd are there any gentlemen who have caught your eye?"

Cassandra laughed as she looked at her cousin.

"I confess I have not allowed myself to even *think* of a single gentleman this evening. I have been much too concerned with making sure that I behave appropriately and do not lose my head when a gentleman compliments me." A slightly embarrassed blush warmed her. "At the first ball, I was determined to think well of everyone who said even the smallest of kind words to me, never considering for a moment that they had underlying, darker motivations. Now, however, I understand that such a thing may very well be so."

"Unfortunately, that may be the case, but not with *every* gentleman." Lady Yardley shook her head, her lips pulling to one side. "I do hope I have not given you the impression that *all* gentlemen are so inclined. In truth, only those who are a little overeager or who have a reputation – whether known to us or not – are the ones to be watchful for... and often, they are the ones who will compliment you from the very beginning of your acquaintance."

Cassandra considered this for a moment, then nodded.

"I do think that is a very wise consideration." Her face began to warm again as she thought of how quickly she had found herself enamored of Lord Darlington, given his flattering manner. "Gentlemen who immediately began to compliment me certainly caught my attention! But perhaps that was their intention all along."

"Perhaps indeed. And some gentlemen may wish to be flattered." Lady Yardley shrugged. "For some, they simply enjoy the attentions of many young ladies. I believe it makes them feel a good deal taller than those who surround them. They think themselves the very best, the most handsome, the most eligible of gentlemen, even though they have no intention of courtship or matrimony."

A slight laugh broke from Cassandra's lips as she recalled how a gentleman named Lord Southwick had done all that he could to compliment her, whilst somehow managing to compliment himself at the very same time. She had not needed Lord Sherbourne's shake of his head to tell her that Lord Southwick was *not* a gentleman to be considered,

"Lord Sherbourne has been a stalwart support to me throughout this evening," she told her cousin. "I am standing up with him for the waltz, in place of Lord Darlington, who was most insistent that I give him what I had promised – though I did so when I did not realize his reputation."

"I am glad that you are relieved from that." Her cousin winced. "There is nothing so disconcerting as dancing with a gentleman who does not concentrate on his steps and seeks only to impress himself upon others – or who seeks to behave in a surreptitious yet inappropriate manner. You need not have any concern as regards Lord Sherbourne, however. He is an excellent dancer."

A spark seemed to ignite itself in Cassandra's heart as she considered Lord Sherbourne, but she quickly doused it and set her gaze on other gentlemen around the room. She reminded herself that Lord Sherbourne had no intention of marrying, and certainly would think her quite ridiculous if she even allowed her thoughts to linger on him for a moment, she pushed his image from her mind. No doubt her cousin would laugh at her if such a thing was ever mentioned!

"I have noticed that Lord Alderton is looking at you." Her cousin glanced at Cassandra and then looked distinctly to her right. "You have noticed him, have you not? He seems to be more than eager for your attention."

All thought of Lord Sherbourne left her as Cassandra's heart suddenly quickened.

"I do not think that we have been introduced."

She glanced at the gentleman in question, and his eyes caught hers for a moment before they darted away again. He was not much taller than her and had a stocky frame, but yet there seemed to be a gentleness about him, for his eyes softened when he smiled. Something in her mind prodded at her and her breath swiftly wrapped itself around her chest – this was the gentleman who had tutted so very loudly and obviously when Lord Darlington had asked about her dowry. Surely that in itself meant he was a good sort!

"Perhaps I should make sure you are introduced." Lady Yardley touched Cassandra's arm lightly. "I know a little of him and to my mind, there is nothing of concern. Lord Sherbourne will know more, mayhap, but we do not need to wait to make introductions." Cassandra considered the man in question, when her attention was brought back to her close surroundings by Lady Yardley's voice. "Ah, Lord Sherbourne. The very gentleman I was looking for."

Cassandra turned her head, as Lord Sherbourne appeared on Cassandra's other side, his hand going to her elbow for a moment.

"Pray do not tell me that you have already found yourself in yet more difficulty, Lady Cassandra?"

Her gaze dropped and she flushed, only to shake her head, giggling alongside his laughter.

"No, I assure you that I have not."

Lady Yardley joined in with the laughter, wrapping one arm protectively around Cassandra's waist as she waggled one finger in Lord Sherbourne's direction.

"Pray do not tease her! She has endured quite enough already."

"Very well, I apologize." With a mock bow, Lord Sherbourne changed his expression to one of seriousness. "Then what is it that requires my aid?"

Lady Yardley tilted her head in the direction of Lord Alderton.

"I wanted to ask your opinion on the gentleman over there. I do not know him particularly well, and thought that you might have a better awareness of his character."

Cassandra glanced over to where Lord Alderton still stood, and their eyes met for a moment before he pulled his away, although she was sure she caught a twinkling smile on the edge of his lips

"You speak of Lord Alderton." The expression on Lord Sherbourne's face was suddenly not one of mock seriousness, for his brows had pulled together and there was a line between them, sending a groove through his forehead. Was there something about Lord Alderton to dissuade her from him? "In truth, I do not know Lord Alderton well." Lord Sherbourne shrugged both shoulders, his gaze still pinned on the fellow. "But what I *can* tell you, however, is –" He stopped short, his eyes narrowing a little and his lips pressed firmly together. What was it he wanted to say and why had he held it back? Given his expression, Cassandra was sure that her hopes would be dashed all over again. Lord Alderton would not be a gentleman she could even *consider*. "I can tell you that...."

For the second time, Lord Sherbourne stopped. This time he cleared his throat gruffly, and Cassandra began to frown. Was he trying to protect her? Trying to keep the truth from her, or find the best and gentlest way he could to tell her the truth about Lord Alderton?

"Lord Sherbourne." Unable to help herself, she took a step closer to him, her eyes now searching his face. "Please."

Lord Sherbourne smiled briefly, but it did not linger – and nor did his gaze.

"I can tell you that I know nothing disreputable about Lord Alderton and his character."

A sudden breath of relief poured from Cassandra's lips. She had not expected to hear those words from him, and a smile slipped across her features the very next second.

"That is not to say that there will be none, however," he continued hastily, as though he wanted to discourage her from thinking anything too exceptional about the fellow. "Again, I would advise caution."

"Yes, yes." Lady Yardley waved one hand. "We need not be so serious. He is only looking and smiling at Lady Cassandra as yet, and many a gentleman has smiled at many a lady before, I am sure."

Again, Lord Sherbourne smiled, but it flickered away in only a moment.

"A few quiet inquiries will be just the thing." Lady Yardley smiled again at Lord Sherbourne and then to Cassandra herself. "What say you, my dear? Shall we go on to introduce you?"

Cassandra looked over at Lord Alderton again. He was not looking at her and she allowed herself a few minutes to study him. He appeared handsome, and there was now the hope that his apparent interest might be reciprocated by her own heart. A handsome, amiable gentleman was what every young lady desired, and there was a small chance that Lord Alderton might be such a fellow for her.

She took in a breath.

"Yes, I should like that very much."

"Very well then."

With a broad smile, Lady Yardley gestured for Cassandra to make her way towards the gentleman, beside her, only for her arm to be caught by Lord Sherbourne.

"Do recall that we are to enjoy the waltz very soon."

A grave expression remained on his face, and Cassandra looked up at him for a long moment, wondering at his strange tone. Was he displeased that Lady Yardley had chosen to introduce her to Lord Alderton? Or was he simply hoping she would not have forgotten the dance she had promised him?

"Yes, I quite recall. I am looking forward to it."

Lord Sherbourne nodded but did not smile. With a parting smile, despite his stern look, Cassandra turned away from him and made her way after Lady Yardley, towards the gentleman in question.

Cassandra took her cousin's arm, hearing her murmur that they would make it appear as though they were simply walking through the ballroom. It took all of her strength to keep her gaze away from Lord Alderton, but after a few moments, her patience was rewarded as a deep voice hailed Lady Yardley.

Cassandra smiled secretly to herself.

"Lady Yardley, might you not introduce me to your new acquaintance? I believe I have met almost all of the new arrivals, save for this fine young woman."

Lord Alderton's compliments warmed Cassandra's heart, but she did not allow herself to overreact. Had she not just learned that every gentleman complimented young ladies very frequently indeed? It was to be expected.

"I should be very glad to." Lady Yardley smiled at him, then gestured to Cassandra. "Lord Alderton, this is my cousin, Lady Cassandra, the daughter to the Earl of Holford. Cassandra, this is the Earl of Alderton."

Cassandra immediately dipped into a curtsey, executing it perfectly, and keeping her head lowered for a moment as she murmured how glad she was to be acquainted with him. The gentleman replied with much the same, and it was only when Cassandra finally allowed her eyes to settle on his that she saw how warm his expression was.

"And are you enjoying the London Season thus far?"

Cassandra laughed immediately, only to see the gentleman's eyebrows lift. A little embarrassed, she quickly attempted to explain herself.

"There is much I need to learn about society," she explained quickly. "I have been in London for some Seasons already with my elder siblings, and have seen things from the sidelines, but to enjoy one's own coming out into society brings with it a good deal more pressure and expectation. I am sure, however, that it will be a most enjoyable time and I will relish every moment."

Lord Alderton blinked and it took a moment for him to smile. Silently, Cassandra cursed herself for being much too open with the fellow, realizing that she had spoken her mind without fully intending to do so. Her nervousness about being introduced to such a handsome gentleman – a gentleman who had been looking at her also – was evidently having an effect.

"I believe you will find that you already exceed expectations, Lady Cassandra." It was another compliment and Cassandra's cheeks blushed lightly as she smiled at him, a little relieved. Thus far, Lord Alderton seemed very pleasant indeed. "And do you have any dances remaining? Or am I much too late?"

Cassandra opened her mouth to say, unfortunately, she had none left, only for Lady Yardley to make a remark.

"I do believe that my cousin only has the waltz remaining, Lord Alderton."

She gestured to Cassandra, who blinked in surprise at the statement. Had she forgotten the waltz was meant for Lord Sherbourne?

"I see." Lord Alderton grinned, his blue eyes suddenly alight. "The waltz, you say? Well then, I –"

"I am afraid this waltz is taken."

Much to Cassandra's astonishment, Lord Sherbourne appeared by her side, his hand pressing lightly through her arm in a somewhat possessive gesture.

"Oh." Lady Yardley's eyes widened slightly in Lord Sherbourne's direction and instantly, Cassandra understood what she had been trying to do. Believing that Lord Sherbourne had only taken Cassandra's waltz to protect her from Lord Darlington, she was now really expecting him to step aside so that Lord Alderton might have it in his stead. For whatever reason, however, it appeared that Lord Sherbourne had no desire to do so. A measure of silence came across the group until Lady Yardley let out a soft sigh, obviously aware now that Lord Sherbourne had no intention of stepping aside. "Forgive me, Lord Sherbourne. I quite forgot."

"Not at all." Lord Sherbourne's voice was quiet and Cassandra did not know where to look, caught somewhere between frustration and an odd thrill at being so desired. "A gentleman will always want to stand up with the lady he has sought out for a dance, will he not, Lord Alderton?"

"Yes, of course. I quite understand." Lord Alderton smiled briefly but did not look toward Lord Sherbourne. "I shall hope for the next time, Lady Cassandra."

Cassandra offered him a quick smile, fully aware of Lord Sherbourne's hand still on her arm.

"Yes, I should be very glad at that, Lord Alderton."

"Then I shall make certain to look out for you at the next ball," came the reply as Lord Sherbourne began to tug her gently away from the group, the music beginning to flood the room already. Becoming a little irritated at Lord Sherbourne's determination, she reluctantly turned away from Lord Alderton, and went with him, doing all that she could to keep her expression calm. He led her to the middle of the room and bowed swiftly, releasing her arm so she might curtsey before stepping forward to take her in his arms again.

"I do not understand why you..."

"I said I would dance the waltz with you, Lady Cassandra." His interruption was somewhat gruff. "Therefore, that is what I am doing."

Cassandra could give no reply, her irritation beginning to fade as his strong hand wrapped around her waist and his other hand grasped hers tightly. The music surrounded them and he began to dance. She followed him easily enough, looking into his face, but he seemingly refused to so much as glance at her, keeping his head turned away. Cassandra bit her lip, a little concerned at his expression, for Lord Sherbourne appeared irritated, if not a little angry, given how tightly his jaw was clenched. Her frustration gave way to concern. Had she upset him in some way? He had been so kind to her thus far, she did not want to injure him.

"I am sure Lady Yardley did not mean to forget."

A small huff of breath came from Lord Sherbourne, his lips curving lightly.

"She did not forget. She simply thought I would step aside so that Lord Alderton could dance with you instead." His eyes finally found hers. "She did not realize, I think, how much I wanted to dance with you myself."

It was as if a flame had been lit within her and Cassandra blinked in surprise at the heat now flooding her. Whatever did he mean by such a declaration? Was it simply a matter of honor? He had written his name there, and thus was intending to stick by it. Or was there something more?

Lord Sherbourne kept his gaze fixed on hers as they danced and, slowly, every other thought began to fade from her head. She could not look away from his hazel eyes, finding glimpses of gold there. The strength of his arm suddenly became much more apparent, his nearness to her sending fresh heat through her frame. Why was she reacting so? Her mouth went suddenly dry as his arm tugged her a little closer. She did not even concentrate on the steps, moving with him as one. He led and she followed.

The music came to a close, but Cassandra was not quite ready to pull herself away from Lord Sherbourne. They stared at each other for a few moments longer, his hand still about her waist and her hand resting on his shoulder. It was only when the hubbub of conversation began to grow that Lord Sherbourne swiftly released her and dropped into a sharp bow. Licking her lips, Cassandra inclined her head and then turned so that she might make her way back to her cousin, relieved to see that Lady Yardley was not gazing out at them.

"Shall we?"

Lord Sherbourne offered his arm and Cassandra took it without a word. She could not find anything to say; the tightness of her chest growing as Lord Sherbourne walked silently beside her. Whatever had taken place, it was so vastly overwhelming, she could not seem to catch her breath. This was nothing like she had ever experienced before and thus, she could make very little sense of it.

"An excellent waltz, Lady Cassandra." Clearing his throat, Lord Sherbourne dropped his head for a moment, keeping his gaze away from her as he deposited her back beside Lady Yardley. "Pray excuse me now. I will seek out a little more about Lord Alderton this evening if I can."

Cassandra nodded, still struggling to know what to say. Her eyes searched his face, but Lord Sherbourne refused to look at her. With another nod, he made to turn away, only for Cassandra to catch his fingers with hers. His head turned sharply, his eyes finally lifting to hers but, immediately after, he pulled his hand away.

"Thank you for dancing with me." Her fingers were warm, her hand burning as she dropped it back to her side. "I enjoyed it very much."

"But of course."

There was a short, sharp response without a smile or a lingering glance and Cassandra's heart twisted painfully, though she did not understand why it was so. As Lady

Yardley began to express more about Lord Alderton, Cassandra allowed her thoughts to linger on Lord Sherbourne, watching him as he walked away. Whatever had happened between them during that waltz, something had shifted within her. Something that, as yet, she could not make head nor tail of – but it lingered there, nonetheless.

CHAPTER NINE

"*A*nd I thought you had an enjoyable evening."

Jonathan rolled his eyes as Lord Knoxbridge sank down into the seat opposite him.

"I had a very pleasant evening, in fact." His eyebrow lifted as Lord Knoxbridge rolled his eyes. "Why would you think otherwise?"

"Because a gentleman does not sit alone with a snifter of brandy in his hand in the middle of White's, unless something unpleasant has occurred." Lord Knoxbridge shrugged his shoulders, tilting his head. "Your expression is not exactly welcoming either."

Jonathan resisted the urge to feign a smile, uncertain as to whether or not he should unburden himself to his friend. Lord Knoxbridge was a fine gentleman in many ways but he could not always be trusted.

"I swear to you, your words are quite safe." Lord Knoxbridge grinned, as though he knew precisely what Jonathan was thinking. "Has someone done something to upset you?"

Rolling his eyes, Jonathan snorted.

"I am not as green as that."

Lord Knoxbridge chucked.

"I am not suggesting for one moment that you are, only that there is something about a situation that now troubles you."

Resisting the urge to roll his eyes to ignore the statement, Jonathan contented himself with a heavy sigh instead, which Lord Knoxbridge dutifully disregarded.

"If you must know, I shall tell you no single person has upset me in any way."

Jonathan threw up a quick smile, hoping that this would put an end to his friend's questions, only for Lord Knoxbridge's eyes to light up.

"Then it is something that *you* have done... or have not done," he declared as Jonathan sighed heavily again. "What did you do? Was it most foolish?" Jonathan was not about to admit to his friend that the cause of his current frustration was his own foolish heart and the way that it clung to Lady Cassandra, so he simply shrugged, picked up his brandy, and took a sip. "Oh, so you will not tell an old friend." Lord Knoxbridge shook his head. "Your silence is a little disappointing. I thought that we were better friends than that."

"Tell me, do you know anything about Lord Alderton?" Changing the subject quickly, Jonathan looked over at Lord Knoxbridge, seeing the flicker of interest which jumped into his eyes, his eyebrows lifting slightly. "Do not ask me why I am enquiring about such things. Will you tell me if there is anything untoward you know about him?"

Someone pushed lightly into the back of his chair – another gentleman who appeared to be a little worse for wear – and Jonathan rolled his eyes, waiting until the fellow had moved away before gesturing to Lord Knoxbridge to answer.

His friend picked up his own glass of brandy and took a sip before he answered.

"Lord Alderton is not a gentleman I know well," he remarked as Jonathan passed one hand over his eyes. "I should think he appears to be a fairly upright sort, for I have never heard anyone say a bad word about his character. He is a quiet fellow, certainly – and to my mind, gentlemen with such quiet dispositions are not generally very good company. So thus, I have not sought out his company very often at all."

Jonathan bit back a laugh, wondering what that said about his own friendship with Lord Knoxbridge. They were two very different sorts, with Lord Knoxbridge leaning towards roguish behavior. Jonathan, on the other hand, enjoyed a few dalliances but never behaved in the way that Lord Knoxbridge did.

"What is your reason for asking about him?"

Shaking his head, Jonathan took another sip of his brandy.

"I did tell you not to ask me the reason...There is a reason, of course. but I am disinclined to tell you what it is."

Lord Knoxbridge chuckled, clearly not taking the remark to be a slant at his character or their friendship.

"Surely I am not as foolish a gentleman as you think me?" His grin grew as he shrugged. "Then again, I suppose that I have let my tongue be a little too loose on more than one occasion."

"Yes, you have," Jonathan threw back at him with a grin. "The only thing I should say is this: it is important that I discover Lord Alderton's true character. However, the fact that he is a quiet sort – as you suggested – sits him in good stead."

Were he honest with himself, Jonathan knew how

eagerly he wanted to find some deeply duplicitous characteristic about Lord Alderton. He wanted to find something despicable, something dreadful and so evil, that it would deter Lady Cassandra from him. That, he realized, was the reason for his dark mood. He did not want Lady Cassandra to be close with any other gentleman, even though he was the one who was meant to be helping her in her quest to find a suitable gentleman – a gentleman who would marry her with love in his heart.

"You are frowning." Pointing this out with one long finger, Lord Knoxbridge grinned as Jonathan narrowed his eyes at him. "There is something difficult going on within your mind, is there not? What is it? Is it about a young lady?" His eyes twinkled. "What is her name?"

Jonathan shook his head.

"I beg of you, do not even *attempt* to guess." A small smile flicked across his lips. "I will admit to you that my thoughts are, at present, settled on a young lady, but it is not as you might believe."

Lord Knoxbridge let out such a bark of laughter, many of the other gentlemen in White's turned their faces to look at him. Jonathan himself dropped his head, highly embarrassed at his friend's laughter.

"Do you truly expect me to believe that you have no particular feelings for any young lady? Even though I am all too aware of just how much you looked at Lady Cassandra this evening?"

Hushing his friend with a hiss of breath, Jonathan shook his head.

"You are mistaken. I was looking at her simply because I have offered to be of aid to her." His voice grew a little louder as his temper rose, and he found himself frustrated at how obvious his behavior had been. "You know very well that I have no intention of matrimony."

"That may be so, but is the lady aware of it?"

Lord Knoxbridge chuckled as Jonathan ran one hand over his face, fighting to keep his anger in check.

"As I have said, I am often in her company, often studying her simply so that I might support her." Struggling in vain to keep hold of his temper, Jonathan slammed one fist down onto the table, aware that he was overreacting, but unable to prevent himself from doing so. "Do you understand me? I am seeking to be the very best sort of fellow I can be so I can support her in her search for a husband." His voice was low, yet filled with an anger that burned through him. "I am thinking of her – and of her friends – so that I can be a support to them and, I might add, to Lady Yardley in her husband's absence." Lord Knoxbridge shook his head, his smile still lingering and it was the smile that frustrated Jonathan all the more. His jaw tightened, his nails biting into the palm of his hand – and yet Lord Knoxbridge simply smiled. "Knoxbridge."

His friend sighed and waved a hand.

"Very well, very well. I shall not ask you any further questions – although you should consider why you responded to me in such a way. That anger is most unusual from you." Holding up both hands, palms out towards Jonathan, Lord Knoxbridge settled back in his chair. "And when you wish to speak about the lady and your unsettling feelings for her, be assured that I will be willing to listen."

Closing his eyes, Jonathan let out a slow breath as his anger began to fade away.

"And speak of it, no doubt." Muttering to himself, and now beginning to feel somewhat embarrassed by his furious reaction, Jonathan threw back the rest of his brandy. "The reason I seek out Lord Alderton's character is to know whether he is a suitable match for Lady Cassandra. I plan to discover whether he is a worthy sort. That is all."

Lord Knoxbridge chuckled again.

"And now the reason for your fury becomes clear." Pushing himself out of his chair, he threw a smile in Jonathan's direction. "When you feel able to discuss such matters with me, then I will be here to talk with you. Otherwise, I wish you well."

Seeing his friend depart, Jonathan bit back his response, deeply frustrated by the fact that his friend seemed to understand more about Jonathan's own heart than he did himself. Settling back into his chair, he scowled to himself, no longer looking after Lord Knoxbridge, but staring straight ahead at the blank wall opposite. These feelings were both confusing and unsettling. He did not want to feel *anything* of what was in his heart, but the feelings ignored his wishes, and were continuing to grow. He had told himself that he would easily be able to remove Lady Cassandra from his thoughts once the shock of seeing her for the first time had worn off. She would only be one of many beautiful young ladies of his acquaintance, and he would not think anything particular of her over any other. Now, however, he was beginning to see that she was going to become a good deal more to him than just a mere acquaintance if he was not careful.

Gesturing for a footman to bring him another brandy, Jonathan closed his eyes and let his head roll back. Thus far, all he was doing was discovering just how much he was beginning to be affected by Lady Cassandra – for, even in his promise to find out the truth about Lord Alderton's character, the hope within him was that the gentleman would prove himself to be unworthy in some way. The more he spoke to people about the fellow, the more he began to fear that his hopes would be dashed. Thus far, Lord Alderton appeared to be a very suitable gentleman indeed. In time, he might come to care for Lady Cassandra and love her as she so desperately wanted to be loved.

But what if I have such a great depth of feeling for the lady myself?

Scowling to himself, Jonathan picked up his brandy and flung it down his throat before settling the glass back onto the table, with perhaps more force than was warranted. Sitting here, lost in thought, was not wise. The best thing for him to do at present would be to leave White's and take himself back to his townhouse. At least there, he would be able to drink a little more and then retire to his bed in peace. He would find no peace here, should he linger.

Pushing himself out of his chair, he made his way to the door, ignoring Lord Knoxbridge's cheery shout of farewell. Someone bumped hard against his shoulder, to the point that Jonathan fell back against the door frame but there was no time to spy who had done so, for someone else was following him closely, as was a third gentleman, and Jonathan had no wish to block the doorway. There were angry voices but rather than turn to find out who had bumped into him, Jonathan shrugged, pushed the annoyance aside, and turned to make his way out of the building.

The street was gloomy, the moon hidden behind thick clouds. For a summer's night, it was very dark indeed. There were one or two lanterns, giving just enough light to make out his carriage waiting for him. Jonathan stumbled towards it, only then realizing that he had drunk a little more than he had estimated. Putting out one hand, he ignored the offer of help from his footman and instead, awkwardly climbed up. Putting one hand on the strap, he hauled himself inside and practically fell into the squabs. Closing his eyes, he rolled his head back, slumping there with his mind still filled with thoughts of Lady Cassandra. He had hoped that the brandy might push her away from his present thinking but thus far, it had not. Her image was still there – a little fuzzy around the edges, but there, nonetheless. He could see her smile; the way that her eyes sparkled when she laughed at something he had said. Was he forever destined simply to be her aid, her support? He desired more, Jonathan admitted, as the carriage began to trundle away, he desired a great deal more - but even that thought was a heavy one. Had he not told himself and his mother only a sennight ago that he had no desire to further his acquaintance with any young lady? He had stated that his mother ought to forget the idea of his marriage. Was he now thinking of such a connection when it came to Lady Cassandra? For whatever reason, thinking of her seemed to make it a distinct possibility – but Jonathan did not want to be connected to a lady in that way... did he?

The carriage came to a stop and with it, his thoughts. Climbing out – and still a little frustrated that his considerations of Lady Cassandra had not lessened, but rather only increased – Jonathan made his way to the house. Stepping inside, he took off his outer coat, hat, and gloves, handing them to the waiting butler, who had not yet retired to his bed, despite Jonathan informing him before he left that he could do so.

"Will there be anything else this evening, my Lord?"

Jonathan shook his head.

"You need not call my valet - I will manage to put myself to bed this evening," he murmured, thinking it would be best to fall into what he hoped would be a dreamless sleep, rather than sit up a little longer. "You should retire also."

The butler inclined his head, although his expression did not change. Jonathan was about to make his way to the staircase, only for the butler's voice to catch his attention again.

"And what should I do with this, my Lord?"

Turning, Jonathan frowned. "What is it?"

The butler handed the piece to him.

"I believe it is a diamond bracelet, the clasp of which appears to be broken. It was in your coat pocket, my Lord."

Taking the item, Jonathan turned it over in his hand as his frown grew. He had very little idea of where this had come from, for he did not recall receiving it or taking it. Had Lady Cassandra given it to him during the evening to keep safe? He could not recall her doing so, but given his somewhat stupefied state, perhaps that was to be expected. Not wanting the butler to think that he did not know of it, Jonathan lifted his chin.

"I had quite forgotten for a moment. Yes, I shall keep it with me."

Saying nothing more, he then made his way to the staircase, the diamond bracelet clutched in his hand. What exactly he would do with it, Jonathan did not know, but such questions could wait until the morning. For the moment, all he wanted to do was forget.

CHAPTER TEN

"And so, we come to our first publication." Lady Yardley smiled first at Cassandra and then at her friends who sat around the room. "It is to go to the printers this evening, and shall be published tomorrow. We already have a great deal contained within it, but there is space for one or two things more... should anyone like to add something?"

Her gaze went meaningfully to Cassandra, who quickly dropped her eyes to her clasped hands. It had been a fortnight since her first meeting with Lord Alderton. They had danced at almost every occasion over these weeks but, as yet, had still not enjoyed a waltz together, despite her attempts. There had been many a conversation, and Cassandra had found herself often in his company. Thus far, Lord Alderton appeared to be charming, amiable, and genteel, as well as rather handsome – but there had been nothing of any importance shared between them. He did appear to be very eager for her company, seeking her out on every occasion that he could, but nothing more had come from him, so far.

Her brow furrowed, recalling the large bouquet of roses which had been delivered earlier that afternoon. The note which had come with it was still etched into her mind, for Lord Alderton spoke of how desperate he was becoming to step out with her for the waltz, bemoaning the fact that he had always been much too late to write his name in that prominent place. Thereafter, he had begged her to write to him to confirm that yes, she would keep her next waltz free for his name and his alone so that his anguish would be no more. As yet, she had not responded to him, but surely such a gesture spoke of *some* sort of interest in her?

"There is a Lord Jefferson." Her face a little red, Miss Madeley spoke up. "He has been paying some close attentions to me. It has been two weeks since our first ball – we danced together that evening – and since then, I have seen him at almost every occasion which I have attended. He always dances with me, speaks with me, and certainly, makes me smile! But there is no indication of courtship as yet."

Her voice wobbled as Cassandra's heart tumbled to the floor. To her mind, it did not appear that Lord Jefferson had any inclination towards committing himself – but mayhap he was only a shy fellow and therefore was acting cautiously. Perhaps he was considering things deeply... or mayhap, he was simply someone who appreciated the attentions of a lady.

"Then I can certainly put in something about Lord Jefferson." Lady Yardley smiled gently. "Though you must be prepared for the difficulty that may come thereafter."

"What shall you write?" another asked, as Cassandra shifted in her chair, eager to know the answer. "What will you say to cause a gentleman to prove himself, one way or the other?"

"It is very simple." Lady Yardley's smile was brief, a slight shadow coming over her eyes. "I shall simply write that Lord Jefferson has often been seen in the company of one particular young lady." One hand went out towards Miss Madeley, who immediately let out a strangled exclamation. "Do not fear, your name will not be mentioned specifically, which is the entire point of a publication such as this."

Lady Almeria nodded slowly.

"I think I understand. You believe that, by stating such a thing, the gentleman will either draw closer or..."

Casting a glance towards Miss Madeley, Lady Almeria hesitated, clearly unwilling to injure her friend.

"Or he will step away from me."

Miss Madeley finished Lady Almeria's sentence as Lady Yardley nodded slowly.

"That is the truth of it, yes. That is why I tell you that you must prepare yourself for some injury. It may come, it may not, but it would not be fair of me to hide the possibility from you."

Cassandra pressed her lips together, seeing how Miss Madeley closed her eyes. Considering for a moment, she began to think on Lord Alderton. There had been no invitations to tea, no afternoon calls, no requests for walks together in Hyde Park, nothing to show his eagerness to further their connection. Yes, they spoke very often and certainly there had been a great deal of delight in their conversations, but none of those conversations had led to something more profound. Was he the same as Lord Jefferson?

After a moment, Miss Madeley lifted her chin and opened her eyes.

"I quite understand and I am prepared."

She lifted her chin and Cassandra's heart sought out the same courage for herself. Taking a deep breath, she caught her cousin's eye.

"Cassandra? Do you have something to add?"

Licking her lips, she nodded.

"Yes, I think I should." Her breath began to quicken but her mind was made up already. "I think I should do something about Lord Alderton. He has shown me some attention, certainly, but nothing of note. Even the note he sent me today did not speak of anything specific with regard to his own intentions. I enjoy his company, and I will confess I find him very handsome indeed." Her friends shared knowing smiles, and Cassandra's face flushed a little. "There is every chance that I could easily find myself in love with him, but I do not want to allow my heart free until it can be sure of his intentions, *and* of his character. If he seeks only a little flirtation, or even a mere friendship, then there is no reason for me to further my time with him."

"Those are wise thoughts, my dear." Lady Yardley smiled gently as though she understood the confusion present in Cassandra's heart. "To be aware that you might swiftly fall in love with such a gentleman is to know yourself – and to be aware of the danger which you might find yourself in, if the gentleman proved to be unworthy, is also well considered. It is always astute to be cautious. I commend you for that."

Cassandra smiled tightly, aware of just how unwise she felt. In fact, she was somewhat frustrated at her lack of good sense. She ought to have immediately mentioned Lord Alderton but had not. It had only been Miss Madeley and her cousin's prompting that had forced her to do so and, whilst she was grateful, Cassandra wished very much that she had come up with the intention herself.

"I shall write something along the same lines as for Lord Jefferson." Lady Yardley's smile faded as a little as concentration steadied her eyes. "In his case, I shall gently suggest that there is more than one young lady interested in Lord Alderton – and such a statement is quite true, for we are *all* interested in him, but only to see whether or not he will prove himself." Her smile returned, glittering now as the young ladies in the room laughed softly, albeit with a slightly nervous air. "To write that will encourage him to prove himself one way or the other, Cassandra." Lady Yardley's voice grew quiet as she looked across at Cassandra again. "You are prepared, I hope, for what might take place once this is published?"

Lifting her chin, Cassandra nodded. Lord Alderton might prove himself to be nothing but a selfish fellow who enjoyed the company of one or two young ladies, without giving his specific attention to anyone in particular. She would have to be prepared for that.

"I am more than prepared, I assure you."

She nodded again as her cousin held her gaze. Yes, she was ready for what would follow, almost eager to discover whether or not Lord Alderton was as he seemed. If he was not, then she would simply have to find herself considering another gentleman, someone who was a good deal more worthy of her time.

And at that moment, none other than Lord Sherbourne appeared in her mind, and Cassandra was filled with nothing but confusion. But yet there he was, lingering in her thoughts, his smiling face soft, his hazel eyes glowing – and Cassandra found herself smiling back as though he were present in the room. The conversation flowed around her, and yet her thoughts lingered on this one gentleman. These last two weeks she had found herself often in his company and certainly had felt some strange sensations rising within her. She had pushed them away quickly enough, however, refusing to allow them to take hold. She would not let herself think of a gentleman who had not only declared himself unwilling to wed but also who had mocked the very idea of a love match. He did not believe in, nor want, such a thing, so why would she ever allow her thoughts to linger on him? Therefore, as she had done so many other times, she pushed him away and tried to center herself once more on the conversation around her.

A quick glance towards Lady Yardley had Cassandra's face flushing, for it was met with a gentle smile and a slight lift of her eyebrow. Did Norah somehow know what she had been thinking about?

Pushing the embarrassment down, Cassandra looked around the room and tried to smile as the other young ladies continued to talk about the gentlemen of London. Try as she might, however, Cassandra's thoughts lingered on the one gentleman she knew she ought *not* to be thinking about.

"I hear you have printed an article."

"Yes." Cassandra lifted her chin, and seeing the flash of Lord Sherbourne's eyes, wondered precisely who - or what - it was directed at. "I felt it was necessary."

Lord Sherbourne's eyebrows lifted.

"But Lord Alderton has no defect with his character, has he?"

Cassandra shrugged.

"You have discovered nothing untoward about him, and nor has Lady Yardley."

"Then why do you seek to write something about him?"

Lord Sherbourne's eyebrows continued to lift until Cassandra thought that they would reach the top of his hairline. "If you are so convinced of his good character, then—"

"Because he has done nothing to show any real interest." The words came tumbling out of Cassandra's mouth as she looked up into his face, seeing his hazel eyes widen a little. "No doubt you will think me foolish, but if I am to lose my heart to a gentleman, I wish very much to know what his intentions are for me, *before* I do so."

Immediately Lord Sherbourne shook his head.

"I should never think you foolish," he murmured, and to her utter astonishment, reached to grasp her hand for a brief moment. "Over the last few weeks, Lady Cassandra, I have come to consider you one of the wisest young ladies of my acquaintance. I do not think that I have ever met someone with such a spirit of determination as you possess."

Cassandra could not speak. The warmth of his hand on hers was sending sparks shooting up through her, her throat constricting a little, but she could do nothing other than look into his eyes. All around them, conversations and laughter continued, and yet to her, there was no one else present save for Lord Sherbourne.

"Lord Sherbourne."

Her voice was soft, throaty, breathless. She did not know what she wanted to say. Was it to ask him to leave his fingers on hers for a few moments longer, or perhaps to ask him to withdraw so that these sensations might stop? Regardless of what she wanted, her words would not come.

"Yes, Lady Cassandra?"

Lord Sherbourne's voice had dropped lower. Was it just her imagination, or had he moved a little closer? Her eyes dropped to his lips. How strange it was that she should be considering them now, wondering what would fire within her should he dare to touch his lips to her own. Her heart quickened, her breathing became uneven as her eyes began to drift closed.

"Alas, it seems we are not to dance this evening." Cassandra's eyes shot open, looking at none other than Lord Alderton. His eyes were fixed on her own, a smile on his lips which she did not feel that she could return. "And here I was, so eager in my desire to dance with you."

Taking a moment, Cassandra forced a smile, wishing beyond all things that he had not interrupted her and Lord Sherbourne.

"Again, it seems we are to be denied, Lord Alderton."

She smiled briefly, glanced at Lord Sherbourne and saw how he had dropped his head. Her heart slammed against her chest as she turned her attention back to Lord Alderton, just as he offered her his arm.

"I am sure you would not mind, Lord Sherbourne, if I stole Lady Cassandra away for a few moments?"

"Certainly I should." Much to Cassandra's surprise, Lord Sherbourne's voice was rather sharp. "You are aware that this young lady ought to be chaperoned. You cannot simply take her through the house without someone being present with you."

"Then how very good it is of you to offer." Was there a hint of ice in Lord Alderton's voice? Cassandra swallowed nervously, worried that there would be some harsh words – but after a moment of hard gazes passing between the two gentlemen, Lord Sherbourne simply shrugged. "Come, my dear." Lord Alderton offered her his arm for the second time, his smile brief as he glanced over his shoulder to where Lord Sherbourne stood. "A few moments of conversation with me and I shall be satisfied."

"Only a few moments?"

Cassandra managed a weak smile, relieved when her remark made him chuckle.

"You want the truth from me? Very well, I shall give it." Smiling, he tilted his head a little closer to her. "I should like to have *all* of your conversations solely for myself, but it would not be gentlemanly of me to ask so." Cassandra glanced away from him, her forehead puckering. Again, there came the sweet remarks, the gentle compliments, but nothing of substance. He had not asked her for her singular company, so that he might enjoy her conversation for a longer time. He had not suggested a walk through Hyde Park, a ride around town or anything that a gentleman would do, were he considering courtship... and thus, Cassandra put barriers around her heart. "You are a little quieter this evening." Lord Alderton looked down at her again, the smile now gone. "I do hope that I have not upset you in some fashion." Catching his eyes for a moment, Cassandra merely smiled but said nothing, giving him no explanation. She could not say anything, could not tell him the truth, and therefore her silence must be her only answer. "You say that your parents are abroad?" Lord Alderton continued after some moments, perhaps thinking that this would be the way to have her converse a little more easily. "Do you miss them a great deal?"

Relieved that he was not going to be asking her anything about her quiet manner, Cassandra quickly fell into conversation.

"Yes, at times."

"Do you know when they might be returning to England?"

She shook her head.

"I write to them on occasion, but even they are uncer-

THE HEART OF A GENTLEMAN | 101

tain as to when they will return. Our letters are infrequent, given the distance."

"I see." His gaze was soft, holding to hers. "You must be very grateful then, for Lady Yardley."

"Certainly I am. She is not only my cousin, but my friend."

"An agreeable situation indeed, then." Lord Alderton smiled. "And your sister is not in London either? Nor your brother?"

Cassandra blinked, a little surprised at his questions. Had they discussed her siblings during their previous conversations?

"My sister is due to go into her confinement within the week, and my brother does not often frequent London, now that he is wed. He is presently at my father's estate, making certain that all is well during my father's absence."

"Then both your brother and your sister are happily situated?"

"As far as I am aware, yes."

"So you have Lady Yardley and Lord Sherbourne to watch over you here in society. It is very good of them both to be so agreeable." Saying nothing, Cassandra resisted the urge to look over her shoulder, to make certain that Lord Sherbourne was still there. Of course he would be. He took responsibilities seriously. "Do you know Lord Sherbourne well?"

Lord Alderton's voice had dropped and Cassandra frowned gently.

"A little, but he has been friends with Lord and Lady Yardley for some time."

Lord Alderton cleared his throat, his head lifting, his eyes fixed straight ahead as though he was not quite certain how to say whatever it was which was on his mind.

"Lord Alderton?" Her steps slowing, Cassandra turned to face him, waiting for him to say whatever he intended – and believing now that it was about Lord Sherbourne. "Is there something wrong?"

He hesitated.

"Nothing is wrong," came the reply, only for a gruff exclamation to follow, as if he were frustrated with himself for not speaking clearly. "It is only to say, I have heard a whisper about Lord Sherbourne which does concern me. Given that he is closely acquainted with you, I would urge caution."

Surprise unfurled like a thorn pressing deeply into Cassandra's heart. Her first instinct was to laugh, for if he was to tell her that the gentleman had no intention of marriage, then she could easily say that such a thing was something she already knew.

"Lord Alderton, Lord and Lady Yardley would not be so close with a gentleman who had anything unscrupulous about his character, I can assure you." She waved her free hand lightly, resuming her walking alongside him. "I am sure that whatever you have heard is nothing short of a dull rumor."

"I should hope it is." Lord Alderton gave a small sigh and shook his head. "I feel duty bound to tell you, however, if you would not mind listening to it?" Giving her no time to answer, he continued quickly. "I have heard it said that Lord Sherbourne has stolen something of great value. I do not know why he would have done so, and my immediate thought is that such a thing is nothing but an untruth. However, there is always the chance that there is more to his character than either you or Lady Yardley might be aware of."

Cassandra looked immediately behind her, but seeing

Lord Sherbourne some distance from them, knew that he had not heard a single word which had been said.

"Lord Alderton, these things are nothing but whispers," she stated firmly. "Lord Sherbourne was, and is, an excellent gentleman. No doubt whoever is saying these things seeks to harm his reputation for some reason. *They* are the ones who should be ashamed, not he."

Lord Alderton nodded, his smile short-lived.

"I must admit to hoping that one day you will be as fervent in your favor of me as you are of him." The smile was now replaced with a heaviness which pushed down his eyebrows and put shadows over his face. "I should return you to Lady Yardley now. I do hope that you enjoy the rest of the evening." Instead of returning her to Lord Sherbourne, Lord Alderton brought her along to where Lady Yardley stood, as though he did not trust to leave her near the very gentleman he had just spoken to her about. Considering that he was attempting to be very kind and cautious, even though she did not think it at all required, Cassandra managed a smile. "Thank you for your time and conversation, Lady Cassandra. Pray think about my words." Only the smallest of smiles flitted across his features. "Good evening."

"Good evening."

Her lips twisting, Cassandra watched him as he walked away, lines beginning to form across her forehead. She had very little understanding of where such rumors came from, but she certainly had no intention of believing them, even if Lord Alderton appeared to be very concerned for her. Why would he be so? Was it because he was afraid that her friendship with Lord Sherbourne might prove to be somewhat disastrous for her reputation?

"Lord Alderton appeared a little brusque, did he not?"

Lady Yardley frowned. "Is he quite all right?"

Cassandra hesitated, just as Lord Sherbourne came to join them. His gaze was fixed on the departing back of Lord Alderton, as though he did not want to take his eyes from him for even a second.

"You had a good conversation with Lord Alderton, then?"

Cassandra tore her eyes away from Lord Sherbourne.

"Yes, I did."

She had the thought, for a moment, of telling them both what Lord Alderton had said about Lord Sherbourne, only to dismiss it. It was far too difficult a possibility, and thus she kept her mouth shut.

"Might I ask what it was that he meant by suggesting that you think about his words?" Lady Yardley's frown lingered. "That seems a little odd... unless-?"

"Yes, I heard that also." Lord Sherbourne finally turned away from where Lord Alderton had been walking. "Did he speak of anything... important?"

Her stomach knotted.

"No, there was nothing of importance as regarded our connection, if that is what you are speaking of."

The light faded from Lady Yardley's eyes, but at the very same time, seemed to fill Lord Sherbourne's expression. Cassandra looked away from them both, suddenly eager to extricate herself. "Ah, there is Lady Almeria. Excuse me, I think I should like to speak with her."

It was just the excuse she needed to step away from them both, her thoughts much too heavy with what Lord Alderton had suggested. Surely it could not be that there was anything wrong with Lord Sherbourne's character? She certainly did not believe him a thief, but where had such rumors come from? And should she tell him of them?

CHAPTER ELEVEN

"*I* need your advice."

Lord Knoxbridge's eyes flared with a sudden excitement as he sat up a little straighter in his chair.

"Are you about to confess to me your feelings for Lady Cassandra?"

Scoffing at this, Jonathan rolled his eyes and let out a bark of laughter, all to hide his immediate sense of embarrassment.

"I hardly think so." So saying, he pulled out the broken diamond bracelet from his pocket and set it on the table. "It is nothing to do with Lady Cassandra. Instead. I need your advice about *this*. It is not mine, you see."

Lord Knoxbridge's eyes widened.

"Why do you have such a thing in your possession if it is not your own?"

Letting out a small sigh, Jonathan lifted one shoulder.

"That is part of the problem. It has been a fortnight since I found this in my pocket – the butler handed it to me, after taking my coat when I returned to my home, and since then I have not known what to do with it."

"I do not understand." Sitting up straighter on his chair, Lord Knoxbridge leaned forward so that he might look at the bracelet more carefully. "Clearly this is an item of great value. Are the diamonds real? They don't appear to be paste, I think."

Briefly touching the bracelet with gentle fingers, Jonathan nodded.

"I assume so."

"And you do not know who it belongs to?"

He shook his head.

"As I said, I found it in my pocket some two weeks ago and since then, have been making some discreet enquiries to attempt to discover who rightfully owns it. First of all, I thought it might be Lady Cassandra's or Lady Yardley's. Neither of them made any remark when I mentioned a diamond bracelet, so it cannot belong to them. There has been no whisper of a lost bracelet amongst society, so therefore I do not know how I am to return it to the rightful owner nor how it came to be in my pocket in the first place."

His lips twisting, Lord Knoxbridge lifted his head.

"And you do not remember everyone present on the evening when you discovered it, I should imagine."

Wincing, Jonathan shook his head.

"No doubt someone gave it to me at some point in the evening – for safekeeping, given its status, and I have quite forgotten about it. My head was a little muddled on one evening, as you may recall. *That* is the night in question."

A broad smile settled across Lord Knoxbridge's face.

"Yes, I recall that – *and* why you were not in the best of situations." His smile faded a little. "Then did someone place it in your pocket that evening?"

"I have no doubt that someone gave it to me for safekeeping; there can be no malevolence there," Jonathan replied firmly. "I do recall dancing with a few young ladies, though I cannot remember all of their names. Perhaps something happened during one of the dances and I was then required to take the bracelet from them. I do not remember it happening however, but that may very well be because..." clearing his throat, he shrugged one shoulder, "I did go on to drink a little at White's."

"At the time when you were trying to convince yourself that you felt nothing for Lady Cassandra." Lord Knoxbridge folded his arms over his chest. "I do hope that you have stopped your pretending now."

"Might you please focus on the question I have asked you, rather than give in to suppositions?" Gesturing to the bracelet, Jonathan threw Lady Cassandra from his mind. "I should like to know your thoughts on what I should do as regards this bracelet, for I must return it to whoever owns it, but how am I ever going to find them?"

Lord Knoxbridge considered for some moments and then, with an unhelpful shrug, sat back in his chair.

"I do not know. Perhaps you ought to have it repaired, in which case someone might then go on to recognize it."

"And mayhap think me a thief." With a frustrated sigh, Jonathan shook his head. "No, I cannot do that. I must be wise and cautious, which requires another way to discover who this belongs to. When I return it, it will be with great caution so that they do not get the wrong impression as to my actions." His face twisted in confusion. "If only I could find out who had put it in my pocket and why they had done so!"

"Mayhap you should ask Lady Cassandra." Lord Knoxbridge's eyes danced. "It may be that she, or one of her friends, will know someone who has lost the bracelet."

Ignoring the way that his heart began to race at the

thought of speaking with Lady Cassandra again, Jonathan merely nodded and turned his face away. His feelings over these last two weeks had increased to the point that it was now entirely disconcerting. The more he tried to push them away, the more intense they appeared to be. Lord Knoxbridge's determination to mention her did not help, for admitting to his affection for the lady was the very last thing that he wanted to do, but the very *first* thing that Lord Knoxbridge sought. While he did not say anything aloud, his inner turmoil only confirmed to him that he was trapped in a whirlwind of emotion, with no simple means of escape.

IT WAS MOST unusual for him to feel nervous in approaching a young lady with whom he was well acquainted. Indeed, Jonathan had been at Lord and Lady Yardley's house on many occasions, but never once had he felt this ball of anxiety rolling through his stomach. Why he should feel it now was beyond his comprehension, particularly as he had done his best to ignore everything Lord Knoxbridge had said to him earlier that afternoon. Even in the carriage ride to the house, he had reminded himself just what it was Lady Cassandra desired – a love match – and how he had no desire for matrimony in the least! He was not ready for such a thing, wanting a few more years of being entirely alone, without responsibility in that regard. Did he not have enough responsibility already? Bearing the title meant duties abounded, and to have a wife in addition to that would surely mean a great deal of expectation settled upon his shoulders. It would bring him pressure and strain, he was sure – given that he had often witnessed how difficult it was for his father to keep his wife in contentment – so therefore, to Jonathan's mind, it seemed wise to live as an unmarried gentleman for just a few more years.

He was rather displeased, then, that his heart rebelled against that idea so fervently.

"I am being foolish."

Speaking aloud to himself, he walked lightly to the drawing room, where he had been directed. Lady Yardley and Lady Cassandra rose at once, having been sitting together, and Jonathan's eyes were once more drawn to the young lady in question.

"Good afternoon, Lord Sherbourne."

He muttered something, his gaze fixed. It was as if Lady Yardley was not present, for the only person he could see was Lady Cassandra. She was wearing a simple light green gown which drew attention to her blue-green eyes, emphasizing the color and evidencing the contrast with her russet head. Jonathan's fingers itched, as though they wanted to run freely through her gentle curls, to feel the softness of her hair, to allow himself the briefest touch against her skin. When Lady Yardley spoke to him again, it took some minutes for Jonathan to realize that there was another voice present.

Blinking rapidly, he forced his eyes away from the vision that was Lady Cassandra, seeing Lady Yardley's lifted eyebrow. Clearing his throat, he tried to find an answer in his blank mind to the question Lady Yardley had presented.

"I..."

Nothing came, and Lady Yardley chuckled softly, as though she knew what his difficulty was. Gesturing to an empty chair, she tilted her head a little.

"Will you sit? You will have to be brief, however, we are expecting company."

"Yes. Of course." Jonathan took a moment, recovering himself slowly as he found a chair to seat himself in. So long as he did not look at Lady Cassandra directly, then his thoughts appeared to be a little less befuddled. "You are expecting company?"

Lady Yardley nodded, her smile remaining.

"Yes, Lord Sherbourne, we are expecting company." She spoke slowly, as if to make sure that he heard her this time. "There have been some gentlemen showing a little more interest in Lady Cassandra's company and, I am sure, particularly after last evening's soiree, that we will have more than a few gentlemen callers! I must say, I thought that Lady Cassandra did very well indeed, would you not agree?"

Giving a small nod, Jonathan clenched his hands into fists, allowing the pain of his fingernails pressing into his palms to give him clarity of mind. There had come a swift kick of jealousy at hearing that gentlemen callers were to be arriving for Lady Cassandra. Neither had he enjoyed last evening, mostly because Lord Alderton had been present, and had taken Lady Cassandra away at a moment where something profound might have occurred... something that, at the time, he had found himself eagerly desirous of. Now, however, Jonathan considered that he was somewhat relieved it had not.

So why, then, am I frustrated with Lord Alderton?

The gentleman had no defect of character and certainly had never treated Lady Cassandra with anything but respect and consideration. All the same, Jonathan's dislike of the gentleman continued to grow. He had been displeased at how Lord Alderton had practically demanded that Jonathan walk behind himself and Lady Cassandra as her chaperone. But having chosen not to argue, Jonathan had done as he had been asked, being forced to watch as Lord Alderton had patted Lady Cassandra's hand and repeatedly dropped his head close to her as they had walked around the room. Even now, his mind told him that he should be pleased that Lord Alderton showed such interest in Lady Cassandra, but his heart continued to rebel against the thought of her being stolen away by Lord Alderton.

"You did hear us, Lord Sherbourne?"

Jonathan's head lifted sharply, as he was pulled from his thoughts.

"I beg your pardon?"

"About 'The London Ledger'? It was published only yesterday." Lady Cassandra's voice was soft. "I am not certain, but I am hopeful that Lord Alderton will have seen what has been written there. I do not know whether he will respond – and, if he does, in what way he will respond – but I can hope that he shall." Her smile lit her expression for just a moment, then faded again. "It may be that he has done nothing but seek my attentions for his own gratification, rather than having any genuine interest in me."

The pain which shone in her eyes had Jonathan flinching. He did not like to see her so.

"I believe it will be the latter."

Those words were spoken from his unwilling lips but, as he spoke them, as he offered her a little hope, Lady Cassandra lifted her gaze to his and smiled softly.

"I do hope so." She looked away again, her smile present for only a moment. "Lord Sherbourne, there is also something I should like to tell you."

The way that her eyes slid towards his, and then shot away again, made Jonathan frown.

"Yes, of course. Whatever is it, I am happy to listen."

Lady Cassandra bit her lip. She did not tell him immediately, and instead of speaking, began to fiddle with something on her lap. Lady Yardley looked just as confused as Jonathan felt, but she said not a word, clearly having no prior knowledge of what the lady wished to say. Jonathan shifted in his chair, seeing how Lady Cassandra glanced at him again before looking away. His heart began to quicken from its usual steady beat. Whatever was the matter?

"It is about something which I was told last evening." The words began to flow from her lips, spoken quickly in an obvious urge to have them free from her. "I shall begin by stating that I have absolutely no intention of believing what I was told, but I do trust that the reason such things were said to me, was simply to make certain that I was aware of what was being suggested."

"I... I do not understand." The tension in his stomach grew, twisting into a knot that pulled back and forth. "You heard something about me?"

"As I have said, it is not something that I personally believe." Swiping the air with her hand, Lady Cassandra held his gaze. "I give you my word on that. In fact, I even told him so, although he appeared less convinced than I was. But that is because—"

The door opened before Lady Cassandra could say anything further, and a gentleman strode into the room, followed by the butler. Evidently, Lady Yardley had stated that all callers were to be brought into the drawing-room without delay and thus, Jonathan had no opportunity to speak to Lady Cassandra further for the moment. Frustrated, he slumped back into his chair as one Lord Litwick began to offer the lady, who had risen to greet him, many compliments.

Catching sight of the brandy in the corner of the room, he rose again quickly, just as Lord Litwick sat, intending to pour himself a small measure. As much as he wished to ignore the fellow, Jonathan could not help but listen to Lord Litwick's many gushing compliments for Lady Cassandra. They flowed from his lips, sounding genuine enough, but Jonathan was quite certain that the gentleman had said such things to many young ladies before. That was not to say that Lady Cassandra would not be affected, however - and it was this thought which had him biting his lip, his frown deepening as he waited for Lord Litwick to draw breath. Would Lady Cassandra believe every word? Would she think him the most handsome and amiable gentleman? Or had she learned by now that not all gentlemen could be trusted? Then again, he considered, taking a sip of his brandy, Lord Litwick might be genuine in his interest and therefore, Jonathan would find himself being asked to look into Lord Litwick's character. Scowling at the thought, Jonathan dismissed the idea, telling himself that Lady Cassandra would not allow herself to be taken in by the gentleman's visit. No doubt Lord Litwick had many young ladies whom he intended to visit this afternoon. Lady Cassandra would merely be the first.

Becoming aware of just how deeply he was scowling, Jonathan quickly rearranged his features and went to retake his seat. There was no reason for him to appear so. Many gentlemen had called on Lady Cassandra during her time in London thus far, why should Lord Litwick be any different? He ought to be pleased Lady Cassandra was being pursued so eagerly! She was beautiful, kind, and amiable. It would be very strange if no other gentlemen in London wanted to become more closely acquainted with her.

But, I want to be the only one who can draw close to her...

The thought made his eyes close as he pinched the

bridge of his nose. Why should he let himself feel such things when he knew they were foolishness? Lady Cassandra was seeking a love match and thus, he was a gentleman who could not give such a thing, for he thought such things were naught but foolishness... did he not?

Unless, he considered, what he was feeling for Lady Cassandra was, in fact, the beginnings of such a thing. Something he had always thought to be the eager thoughts of young ladies in their first Season, and nothing more – could it be, now, that it was sinking into his soul?

He threw back his brandy in one gulp, just as Lord Litwick refused any more tea and stated that he had to take his leave. Much to Jonathan's relief, the room was, once more, free of the fellow and only the three of them remained. Rising to his feet, Jonathan came over to where Lady Cassandra was finishing sipping her tea, Lady Yardley sitting opposite, making sure to leave his thoughts in the chair behind him.

"Lord Litwick was very complimentary." Sitting down in a chair next to Lady Cassandra, Jonathan lifted an eyebrow as she giggled. "You do not think so?"

"If you are concerned that I will be overcome by Lord Litwick's compliments, then you need to not be." Lady Cassandra shook her head. "He is a gentleman who is most inclined towards speaking well of people, but does so at such great lengths, it leaves him with very little to say other than that. Besides which, he did not permit me to say very much in return!"

Jonathan found himself chuckling, somewhere between relief and mirth over Lord Litwick's behavior. How good it was to know that the fellow had not left a lasting impression! He could not allow himself to express that relief, however, for with it might come with some expression of his own feelings – feelings which, as yet, he could not fully comprehend.

"I am certain that, if he is genuine, he will return to you, Lady Cassandra. You deserve every compliment he offers." He took a breath. "And many more, in fact."

The surprise which filled Lady Cassandra's eyes was reflected in Jonathan's own heart. He had not intended to speak so openly, but those words lingered in the air between them. He waited for the pang of regret to fill his heart, but none came. It was as if a part of him was glad of how he had spoken, relieved that he had been honest about what he thought of Lady Cassandra. He had surprised her, and himself, but no remorse followed.

"I- I thank you. You are very kind to say such a thing."

Jonathan shrugged, muttered something, and then threw a glance toward Lady Yardley, a little surprised to see a small smile on her lips. There was no flicker of surprise lingering in her expression, as though she had expected him to speak in such a manner and was now glad that he felt free enough to do so. Mayhap, he considered, she smiled for Lady Cassandra, eager for her courage to be bolstered, and knowing that his words were honestly meant, rather than being spoken with any selfish motivations.

"Now." Jonathan coughed lightly, trying to recall what it was that he wanted to speak to Lady Cassandra about. "Before Lord Litwick arrived, there was something you wanted to tell both myself and Lady Yardley, was there not?" A frown pulled at Lady Cassandra's forehead, and she caught one finger between her teeth. Jonathan studied her carefully, for it appeared as though she had forgotten what she wanted to say - only for him then to realize that it was, in fact, quite the opposite. It was not that she had forgotten, but rather that she was concerned about what it was she had to say. Such concern kept her lips sealed but her eyes darting between himself and Lady Yardley. "Do not be worried in any way." Aware that Lady Yardley was still very much present, Jonathan could not help but reach out to touch Lady Cassandra's hand lightly, as it rested on the arm of her chair. "Speak honestly."

"Lord Sherbourne is right." Lady Yardley's expression was also one of concern, for her lips were thin and her eyes fixed to Lady Cassandra's. "There is nothing you can say which will either upset or anger us. We shall only be relieved that you have told us whatever it is that is troubling you at present."

"Please."

Her fingers were soft and warm under his and much to Jonathan's delight, as he spoke, they eventually curled around his own.

"As I have said, I do not believe what I was told." Again, Lady Cassandra bit her lip. "I do not believe a *word* of what has been said. In fact, I am upset that such things have been suggested about you."

Jonathan curled his fingers tighter.

"You heard things about me?"

She nodded, her eyes a little wide.

"I believe that this was told to me out of concern for me." Her shoulders lifted a little. "Of course, I told Lord Alderton that I did not believe him but, all the same, he did appear to be rather troubled."

"Lord Alderton told this to you?" Jonathan blinked as Lady Cassandra swallowed, turned her eyes away, and nodded. Something about this was already deeply unsettling. It was not only the fact Lady Cassandra had heard something disturbing about him, but also that Lord

Alderton was the one who had spoken of it. "I am afraid you shall need to explain."

He did not remove his hand, and nor did she loosen her grip. Instead, they simply held onto each other as Lady Cassandra drew in a breath.

"Lord Alderton, my Lady."

The door opened and Jonathan swiveled his head, quickly releasing Lady Cassandra's hand, but not before Lord Alderton had stepped inside, his eyes going immediately to where Jonathan and Lady Cassandra's fingers had been connected. There was no embarrassment in Jonathan's heart, however, no hint of shame. Instead, he found himself almost glad that Lord Alderton had walked in to find them so. It was a laughable thought and Jonathan knew that he ought to regard it as foolish, but instead, he simply smiled as the gentleman inclined his head.

They all rose, and as Lord Alderton bowed, Lady Yardley spoke.

"Good afternoon, Lord Alderton." Lady Yardley gestured to an empty chair. "Please, do come and join us."

She settled back into her chair, and Jonathan also sat, Lady Cassandra resuming her seat beside him.

Instead of doing as was asked, Lord Alderton merely folded his arms over his chest and looked directly at Lady Cassandra. The severity of his gaze surprised Jonathan somewhat. Did he really think that he had any authority here? Did he believe that he could somehow demand how Lady Cassandra behaved? Such expectations were foolishness. They were not even courting, so therefore the gentleman had no right to demand anything from the lady.

"You apparently have not taken heed of my warning. Lady Cassandra."

The gentleman spoke with such an authoritative tone

that Jonathan lifted both eyebrows. He was about to say something, about to set Lord Alderton back a step, only for Lady Cassandra to speak first.

"As I have said to you, Lord Alderton, I do not accept your concern as my own." She pressed her lips together for a moment as Lord Alderton's frown grew. "Mayhap you think it foolish, but I do not believe for a moment that Lord Sherbourne is a thief."

"A thief?" Jonathan repeated, his chest tightening as Lord Alderton nodded, his arms still folded tightly across his chest. "And *you* are the one to say this, Lord Alderton? How dare you impugn my honor?"

"*I* do nothing of the sort." Lord Alderton flung out both hands in Jonathan's direction. "But what if a young lady's reputation should be damaged by her association with a gentleman who has such deep and dark rumors associated with him? What else is there for me to do but warn the lady?"

"I have never heard anything so preposterous." Lady Yardley shook her head, her face a little flushed. "I can understand that your intentions were good, Lord Alderton, but such rumors ought to be ignored. There is no truth in them. I do not even need to hear them to know that."

Jonathan lifted his chin, attempting to hold back the rising tide of anger. He was trying his best to see the good in Lord Alderton and his attempts to protect Lady Cassandra but, at the same time, his ire was beginning to bubble so furiously, he wanted to direct it at someone – and Lord Alderton seemed the very person to whom he must throw it.

"I have never stolen anything in my life. I would hope that a gentleman such as yourself would put an end to such rumors by simply ignoring them. Or, in fact, stating to whoever it was that told you, that their accusation must be proven to see if it holds even a single speck of truth."

His words were harsh and tight, spinning from him like darts, but Lord Alderton remained unmoved, his dark expression fixed.

"And what if the person I spoke with told me that they could prove it?" The gentleman's voice had dropped low, and a sudden sense of foreboding ran straight through Jonathan's frame. "What if I had already said the very thing to them that you have just stated? Then, Lord Sherbourne, what should you do?"

"I should still think it to be absurd, and that the person telling you such rumors must have made a mistake." Lady Cassandra spoke before Jonathan himself could respond. "As I have told you, Lord Sherbourne, I have never believed a single word of this. In fact, I told Lord Alderton the very same thing. Not a word of it can be believed, even if it can *supposedly* be proven, I am still not inclined to believe it."

"Very well." Lord Alderton shrugged. "Then, Lord Sherbourne, I assume that you do not possess a diamond bracelet? One where the clasp is broken, one that has such great monetary value that it is very rarely worn outside of the home for fear of its loss? Will you stand here and tell both myself, Lady Cassandra, and Lady Yardley that you do not have that item in your possession?"

Everything within Jonathan began to burn in one single moment. His entire body was on fire, every muscle tense as his anger began to blow away like smoke. Somehow, Lord Alderton had found out about the situation with the bracelet and he was now using it to his advantage. Jonathan closed his eyes briefly, as the image of Lord Knoxbridge's face entered his mind. There was no doubt that his friend was the one responsible for this, for he was the only one he had spoken to - but that was not the issue at present. How was he to prove himself? Should he state that he had absolutely no knowledge of what Lord Alderton spoke of? Or should he confess the truth to Lady Cassandra and explain himself thereafter?

"Lord Sherbourne?"

There was a slight quiver to Lady Cassandra's voice as she spoke his name. Jonathan looked towards her, his heart quickening into a fast, furious pace. He did not know what to say; the choice laid out starkly before him.

"Cassandra, I–"

"I should like to know the name of the person you have been speaking with, Lord Alderton." It was Lady Yardley's voice that interrupted the quiet, giving Jonathan a few moments to collect himself. "And why has this person not come to speak to Lord Sherbourne directly?"

"That is a private matter."

Lord Alderton's response confirmed to Jonathan that the person he had spoken to was none other than Lord Knoxbridge.

"Then it is all just hearsay," Lady Yardley continued, sharply. "You have no proof of what you have said – and therefore, it is unfair of you to demand anything from Lord Sherbourne." There was a hardness in her tone, her features almost carved into stone. "Rather, you should have come to speak gently, informing Lord Sherbourne of this rumor, instead of insisting that he prove himself one way or the other."

"I speak only out of concern for Lady Cassandra." Lord Alderton sent sharp eyes toward Jonathan, who simply continued to watch the interplay, still battling with feelings of anger, concern, and confusion. "I speak as someone who does not want her reputation to be damaged in any way."

"Which is very kind of you, but that responsibility ultimately falls to me." Lady Yardley rose from her chair, her strength obvious in her stance and flashing eyes. "As a gentleman who has not proven himself to be anything more than an acquaintance to my cousin, albeit one who seeks out her company, I find your concern rather... misplaced."

Rather than respond with any apology, Lord Alderton's eyes narrowed a little.

"You speak of what has been written in 'The London Ledger'," he shot back, his sharp tone now matching that of Lady Yardley's. "First of all, I should state that I do not read publications such as that, but it was mentioned to me that my name was within it. The Ledger states that several young ladies are interested in my company and I in them. The first part of the statement may well be true, but why that should make you question my concern for Lady Cassandra is a little confusing, Lady Yardley."

Lady Yardley took a breath, her hands going to her hips but it was Jonathan who responded first, no longer able to remain silent.

"It is mentioned because you have never made any commitment to Lady Cassandra, even though your acquaintance is a strong one." He shrugged as Lord Alderton scowled. "You do appear to be very eager for her company, and I cannot blame you for your interest - but if there are many young ladies interested in your company also, many young ladies to whom you are offering your attentions, then one might question why you have never taken your acquaintance with Lady Cassandra any further, if you are in any way serious. Those words in 'The London Ledger' simply seem to prove that you are a gentleman willing to give your interest to many a young lady, but to make your commitment to none."

Lord Alderton lifted his chin.

"Then I shall prove myself immediately." Turning to Lady Cassandra, he inclined his head for a moment. "Lady Cassandra, I very much enjoy your company. I find you an excellent young lady with an amiable heart and think you most beautiful. I should very much like to ask you to take walk with me, come the morrow. In fact, I invite you to take tea with me first and then perhaps, take a drive in the phaeton to Hyde Park, so that we might walk about the park during the fashionable hour." His sidelong gaze caught Jonathan's. "Perhaps that will be enough to prove my seriousness in this matter not only to you, but also to Lord Sherbourne."

Jonathan's stomach dropped. This was not what he had expected to hear from Lord Alderton. Lady Cassandra, however, was looking from Jonathan to Lord Alderton and back again, her face pale, and confusion in her eyes.

"I - I do not know what to say." Her hand pressed to her eyes for a moment. "Of course, I am grateful for your invitation, Lord Alderton, but at the same time, I cannot allow my thoughts on Lord Sherbourne's character to be so confused. I do not think that I could be contented in walking with you, knowing that you think so little of him. Lord Sherbourne has done nothing but prove himself to me over and over again, so I know him to be a gentleman of the highest order. This evident disdain for him, this concern over his character, and your belief that he is a thief, does not align with my own opinion. Therefore, as much as I would like to accept, I–"

"There is no need to do such a thing, Lady Cassandra." Jonathan spoke quickly, desiring the situation to come to an end, but at the same time aware that he could not permit Lady Cassandra to push herself away from what could be the sort of match she was looking for. As much as he disliked Lord Alderton, as much as he believed him wrong to have brought up such an accusation, it did not mean that he was not the right gentleman for Lady Cassandra.

Even though I wish to be the one for her...

His heart twisted, but he forced himself to continue speaking in the same manner.

"Lord Alderton is speaking in an attempt to protect you, which I understand. It is a little misguided, but that does not mean that he is wrong to do so." Finding that he could not even look at the gentleman in question, Jonathan kept his gaze fixed only on Cassandra, all too aware of how painfully his heart was beating. It was screaming at him, begging him not to push her towards the other man, and yet, the words continue to flow from his mouth. "Do not hold back from Lord Alderton on my account."

Lady Cassandra took in a shuddering breath. Her eyes squeezed close, and she shook her head.

"It is not only that, Lord Sherbourne." She looked at him again, tears beginning to glisten in the edges of her eyes. "There is something –"

"I think that what *you* should do, Lord Sherbourne, is inform us all whether or not you have that particular bracelet." Lord Alderton interrupted them all, moving to stand in the center of the room, his hands at his sides, but his eyes fixed in Jonathan's direction. "And I think that you should confess it *before* Lady Cassandra feels the need to comment further. Perhaps you would do us the honor of being truthful."

Jonathan blinked rapidly. There was something different in Lord Alderton's tone this time. Mayhap Lord Alderton was *not* a gentleman who was only concerned about Lady Cassandra. Could it be there was something more here? Something deeper, something darker?

"As Lady Yardley has said, it is not right for you to demand anything from me." He rose from his chair, afraid that, by saying nothing, he was revealing his guilt. "If you think that you can stand there and insist that I am a thief and second of all, demand that I prove it, then you are quite mistaken."

Lord Alderton's eyes glittered.

"So you are in possession of it."

"Whether I am or not, you can be assured that I am no thief." Keeping his voice steady and his eyes fixed, Jonathan drew in a long breath, settling his shoulders as he did so. "I think that the time has come for me to take my leave." With a short bow, he looked first to Lady Yardley and then to Lady Cassandra. Her eyes were still brimming, but she was not looking at him any longer. Instead, her attention was turned to Lord Alderton... and at that moment, Jonathan feared that she was slipping from him. Everything he had pretended he did not want was being taken away, and even though he had told himself, over and over, that he did not even want to give his heart to Lady Cassandra, his heart suddenly cracked, sending pain ricocheting through him. Without another word, without another glance in her direction, Jonathan strode from the room, bearing more pain than he had ever felt in his life before.

CHAPTER TWELVE

"*A*re you quite prepared?"

Cassandra dared another glance at her reflection in the mirror on the wall of the drawing-room, aware of how pale she appeared, how her lips did not smile at the thought of walking with Lord Alderton in Hyde Park. She had declined his invitation of taking tea and taking his phaeton to Hyde Park but had stated that she would be glad to walk with him for a short while during the fashionable hour. It was the first time that he had made any sort of obvious indication of his serious interest, but she could not get the previous afternoon's altercation from her mind. She had not seen Lord Sherbourne at the previous evening's soiree - even though she had expected him to be there - and he had not so much as sent her a note. Lord Alderton had been quite convinced of Lord Sherbourne's guilt and had declared it so without seeming to realize how much of a dagger he was stabbing into her heart.

"You need not walk with him if you do not wish to." Lady Yardley settled a hand on her shoulder. "If you do not like the gentleman particularly well, then why should you concern yourself?"

Cassandra sighed as she looked at her cousin.

"It is not that I do not like him." Taking a breath, she spread her hands. "I believe, as you do, that he told me of such rumors because he is concerned for me, and for the company I keep. He thinks of my reputation rather than anything else and thus, I should be grateful. However, the fact that he said such a thing about Lord Sherbourne is rather difficult for me to accept, especially when..." she trailed off, her heart aching so terribly, it was a constant pain in her chest.

"Especially when there appears to be a possibility that what Lord Alderton has said is true."

Lady Yardley's lips twisted, and Cassandra could not help but nod. Yes, that was her concern - for while Lord Sherbourne had refused to answer the question presented by Lord Alderton, she had seen how pale he had turned and how his eyes had dropped – to the point where she was now afraid that there was a hint of truth in Lord Alderton's accusation.

"If Lord Sherbourne had come to speak with us, if he had even written a note, then I would not feel so concerned." Sighing, she shook her head. "But given that he has done neither of those things, I feel myself a little lost. I do not want to believe the accusation that he has taken the diamond bracelet, but his words did seem to imply otherwise."

Lady Yardley nodded, her lips pursing for a moment.

"He stated that he was not a thief, whether he has the bracelet or not. We should be able to trust his word in that. Perhaps it is not as Lord Alderton thinks, for it may be that while Lord Sherbourne has the bracelet in his possession, he has not taken it for himself."

"Then why has he not explained his reason? Surely he must know that we are confused."

Her heart turned over as Lady Yardley shook her head.

"I do not know why." Taking a breath, she smiled warmly, her gaze steady. "What I *can* say is that I know Lord Sherbourne very well. I have known him for years – and my husband even longer, for they have been close friends since Eton!" She smiled. "My husband has always chosen his acquaintances carefully, even from a young age. If there was any sort of unsavory behavior in Lord Sherbourne's past or even his present, I can assure you that my husband would have found out about it, and certainly would have informed me also. We are not the sort to keep secrets from each other. I can promise you that Lord Sherbourne is exactly as he appears – a good-hearted fellow, with kindness and responsibility at the core of him. If he says that he is not a thief, I would urge you to believe him."

Cassandra's mouth lifted a little, her cousin's words soothing the fragmented thoughts which dug furrows into her heart. It seemed that she was not to be given any answers from Lord Sherbourne at present, which meant that she would have to wait until he presented the truth to them.

And as for Lord Alderton?

Sighing, Cassandra closed her eyes. Truthfully, she had no real desire to walk about with Lord Alderton this afternoon, had no thought of laughing or smiling or enjoying herself with him, not when her heart remained on Lord Sherbourne alone. She did not want to even think about what it would be like if Lord Sherbourne left London - but rumors such as this could easily drive a fellow from society.

If word went around London that Lord Sherbourne was a thief, then would he return to his estate, rather than stay and battle the rumors? She could not blame him if he chose the former rather than the latter, but all the same, the thought of being in London without him became a heavy burden to bear.

"Should I inform Lord Alderton that you are not particularly well this afternoon?" Lady Yardley searched Cassandra's face. "I am sure that he will understand."

Cassandra shook her head.

"No, I should not like to do so. I have spent a long time waiting for him to commit himself, to say whether he will be willing to choose me or not – and now he has seemingly done so, it would not be right of me to ignore him."

Lady Yardley smiled in understanding.

"Very well." Her hand fell from Cassandra's arm. "I know that you are concerned about Lord Sherbourne, but do try not to allow him into your thoughts when you are with Lord Alderton. The publication of 'The London Ledger' appears to have done what we hoped for since Lord Alderton now seems to have decided to show you a keener interest, and such interest may very well lead to courtship if all goes well. If you do not allow your thoughts to linger on Lord Sherbourne, then you will surely have a pleasant afternoon."

Cassandra nodded, and tried to smile, but did not manage to do anything other than a faint lift of one side of her mouth.

"I will do my very best to do so."

She had no real joy in the prospect of walking with Lord Alderton and, even now, the talk of courtship did not thrill her. She had thought she would be able to allow her heart to be free, to be ready to fall in love with a gentleman who declared himself in the way that Lord Alderton had done, but now Lord Sherbourne was such a burden on her mind that she could think of none but him, despite her cousin's encouragement.

"Are you quite sure?"

As though she were able to read Cassandra's thoughts, Lady Yardley asked her again but, this time, Cassandra met it with a nod of her head and quick steps towards the door.

"Yes, I am quite certain."

So saying, she opened the door and made her way through the hallway to the front door where the carriage was waiting. This could be the first step into her future, she told herself, the beginning of the love match which she so desperately wanted. All the same, her hands tightened in her lap, her forehead continued to frown, and her eyes remained fixed on a point ahead of her as she sat in the carriage. She was still thinking of nothing but Lord Sherbourne and, despite the fact that Lady Yardley kept up a stream of cheerful conversation as the carriage made its way to Hyde Park, Cassandra found that she simply could not join in. Would Lord Sherbourne be at Hyde Park? Would he offer her the truth of what had happened with the diamond bracelet, or was their last conversation to be the only explanation she would ever have?

LORD ALDERTON WAS WAITING for her to emerge from the carriage, the sunlight gleaming off his brown hair. The broad smile on his face told her that he was not thinking of their last conversation. In fact, when she approached him and he immediately began to speak of how fine an afternoon it was, she realized that he had already set aside that conversation completely. She was still caught up with it however, despite the fact that she had told her cousin she fully intended to do as much as she could to enjoy her time with Lord Alderton. Just seeing Lord Alderton again brought that entire situation back to mind, recalling how differently he had appeared, with his hands clamped to his waist, his stance wide, and his eyes flashing. Compared to how he was now – his smile gentle, his forehead unlined – it was as if she were in the presence of a different gentleman entirely.

"I cannot tell you how glad I am that you agreed to walk with me." Lord Alderton offered her his arm, and she accepted it. "Hyde Park is not particularly busy as yet, but soon it will become very crowded, I am sure. The fashionable hour is not upon us but it is not far off, and I will be very glad for gentlemen and ladies alike to see you on my arm." Cassandra glanced over at him, then nodded, but did not say anything by way of agreement. "Might ask if you are a little upset about what you read in 'The London Ledger'?" His frown drew lines into his forehead. "I do not read papers such as that myself, as I may have said before, but it was brought to my attention, and I am concerned about what you thought of it."

She turned her head to catch his eyes, then pulled her gaze away again, for his look was much too intense. The way that he was studying her spoke of genuine concern, as though he was truly worried about what she would think of him.

"I suppose...," she began slowly. "I suppose I should not be surprised that there are other young ladies interested in your company. It was an explanation for your lack of... focused interest in *our* acquaintance, which I had not previously considered."

Lord Alderton huffed out a breath.

"You thought that, because it seemed that I had so many young ladies eager for my company, you might only be one of many I sought out?" The dark tone which flooded his words sent a flash of guilt through her, as though she should know that she was the only one he considered. Warmth began to push up into her face and she dropped her head. "I should take the blame upon myself." Lord Alderton shook his head and sighed loudly. "I was not as obvious as I ought to have been."

Cassandra swallowed.

"It is not your fault that many young ladies are eager for your company, I think."

Her cheeks flushed as she spoke, well aware that this was something which Lady Yardley herself had written in 'The London Ledger' as a mere whisper rather than as having any foundation in truth. The way that Lord Alderton was responding, however, it seemed that what had been written about him, he considered to be quite true. Perhaps she *was* only one of many young ladies whom he sought out on a fairly regular basis. Had she been foolish to hope otherwise?

"That may very well be true, Lady Cassandra, but that does not mean that I could not have made myself a good deal clearer before this moment." Clearing his throat, he turned to face her so that they paused in their walk. "In fact, I should have explained my position to you before now. Forgive me for the delay. I shall do so now if I might?"

Cassandra swallowed, then nodded.

"Please."

Lord Alderton lifted his chin and straightened his shoulders.

"Lady Cassandra, I am a gentleman who takes his time in all things. I contemplate everything with great care before I make a decision. It is a trait that has proven valuable to me a good many times thus far in my life. Therefore, Lady Cassandra, I confess to you that I *am* thinking about you, and our potential future together, but I must do so with careful consideration. I have many requirements and must make certain that whoever I wed will be the most suitable for both myself, my future heirs, and my estate. However, I do think that your gentle nature, sweet spirit, and obvious beauty are a fitting match for me."

Cassandra blinked. He had not mentioned a single word about emotion. There was not even a small suggestion that he might find himself in love with her, as she had been hoping for. In fact, all he had mentioned thus far was practicality, although, of course, he had been most complimentary about her in doing so. But such words did not mean that there was any hope of affection. If there was not even the smallest hint of it, then what was she to do? Cassandra had no doubt that her future would look rather dark if it was without love.

"Ah...."

She made an indeterminate sound, indicating that she had heard his words, and hoping that doing so might encourage him to say more.

"It was not until I was told about what was written in the paper that I realized I had to make a decision." Lord Alderton shook his head, speaking through her confusion. "Forgive me, Lady Cassandra. I have taken far too long to make a choice. I certainly should have asked you to walk with me or even to take afternoon tea together, long before this moment. It has been almost three weeks since we were first acquainted, and such a length of time is *more* than long enough to consider what one might want for one's future." So saying, Lord Alderton settled one hand over hers for a moment, though his gaze remained locked upon hers, as though she would hope to see the fervency in his eyes. "I can only apologize for the confusion and doubt that you must be feeling. I have every intention of taking our close acquaintance seriously. It is consideration and caution which have held me back until now – and I recognize that perhaps I have been overly careful."

He smiled at her, but Cassandra was not quite able to return it. Her heart was beating a little more quickly but it was not from excitement, nor the thrill of what he had said. Rather, she found herself struggling with disappointment. Lord Alderton had not mentioned love nor even affection, speaking only of how he required a wife who would fit into every area of his life and his estate. But that was not what she wanted! That was not what she was looking for, not what she desired from their courtship. To be seen only as someone suitable rather than someone he could not do without, would not bring her any happiness.

"From your silence, I begin to think that I shall have to prove myself to you." Cassandra merely smiled briefly as she began to walk again, silently thinking that yes, he *would* have to prove himself to her, for if he did not want love to be a part of their acquaintance, then she did not want to be acquainted with him. It was as simple as that. "Now I fear that I have made you melancholy." Lord Alderton stopped, swung around, and grasped both of her hands in his so that she had no other choice but to look up into his face. His eyes were searching, his expression serious, looking for answers which only she could give. "You do appear to be a little unhappy this afternoon. If you would tell me of it, I would be glad to know of your concern, in the hope that I can remedy it in some way."

Cassandra considered for a moment. If she was to be

honest with Lord Alderton, then she would tell him of her desire for a love match. If she was not, then she would simply have to hope that such a thing might flourish within their connection. Recalling the pact which she had made with her friends, Cassandra took a moment to draw her courage together, deciding to speak honestly.

"I am not at all upset with your company, Lord Alderton," she began, truthfully. "I will confess that seeing what was written in 'The London Ledger' has provoked me. I had thought, given how often we were in company together, that you and I might have a specific connection, unshared with others – but I fear that I have been foolish in that regard."

"No, you have not." To her astonishment, Lord Alderton drew closer, his hands squeezing hers as his fingers sought to lace through her own, even though Lady Yardley was standing only a short distance away. There was a gleam in his eyes, his breath rushing across her cheek as he spoke urgently. "You are not foolish, I assure you. I can see now that *I* am the one who has been so. There is only one young lady I want to consider and she is standing here before me at this very moment."

Taking a deep breath, Cassandra was about to let herself smile, only to hesitate. Yet again, he had not spoken about love, had not even mentioned a fondness for her. Why would she then be glad of his attention? No, even in this, she could not allow her heart to be silenced. The gentleman did not seem to even *consider* love and thus, she had to draw back from him.

"You speak well, Lord Alderton." Glancing at Lady Yardley and seeing her cousin watching the display with sharp eyes, Cassandra dragged in another breath. "You speak only of what – or who – would be the best for your situation, and whilst I understand that a suitable match is the desire of many a gentleman, I myself do not seek only that. I have no desire for a marriage of practicality."

At this, Lord Alderton immediately frowned as one hand let go of hers.

"Then what is it that you seek, Lady Cassandra?"

The heat in her cheeks began to rise as she took in a deep breath.

"Lord Alderton, I seek, at the very least, a genuine affection." She did not go so far as to speak of love, quite certain that it would turn the gentleman away from her entirely. "The simplest way to explain it is to state that I do not want to go into a marriage where there is only a consideration of each other's suitability as regards the role of husband and wife, with no concern for affection. You may find this rather ridiculous or even foolish, but it is the standard that I am determined to follow."

Lord Alderton stared at her for some seconds without saying a single thing. He did not blink, did not even seem to breathe, given the stillness of his frame, and Cassandra felt herself shrinking inside. Did he think her truly absurd? No doubt it was not something he had expected to hear from her, given she was the daughter of an Earl, who would have been schooled in just how suitable a match she had to make. And yet Cassandra could not bring herself to accept that sort of marriage.

"Good gracious."

Cassandra's stomach dropped to the ground, only to throw itself back into position as Lord Alderton began to smile. Instantly she recoiled from him, but his hands tightened a little more on hers.

"I am not laughing at you," Lord Alderton said hastily, his eyes now soft rather than filled with confusion. "I swear to you, Lady Cassandra, I do not have a single flicker of mirth in my heart at present. It is only to state that my admiration of you has been strong, but in hearing you speak so, that admiration has now redoubled itself. I did not think I could admire you more, Lady Cassandra, but it seems I have been proven wrong."

Letting out a shaking breath, Cassandra looked away from him, uncertain as to the meaning of his reaction. Again, he did not speak of affection, neither agreeing nor disagreeing with her and what she had said. Yes, he had spoken about his admiration, but his admiration was not what she sought.

"Come, let us walk again." Lord Alderton offered his arm, and she took it almost without thinking, glancing over her shoulder towards Lady Yardley, who gave her a small nod, encouraging her to continue. "Just as you have been truthful with me, I shall be truthful with you." Lord Alderton cleared his throat, no smile on his face now. "I am a gentleman who has always been practically minded, as I have just said. It must be so, for my estate requires an heir and, therefore, I have always thought about my future bride in terms of suitability. Perhaps it was a mistake, but it is what is expected. I have never even *allowed* myself to think about affection or love. If I can find a creature who is quite beautiful and of the proper standards, then I will consider her."

Something like a heavy stone sank into Cassandra's stomach as she nodded slowly, understanding what he was saying but finding herself disagreeing in every possible way. She could never consider a gentleman simply because of his standing. It simply would not bring her heart any contentment.

"I see."

"If I am honest, however, I should say that there have

been some... strange feelings beginning to encroach upon my heart." Lord Alberton shook his head and turned it away so that he could not look at her. When Cassandra glanced at him, she saw a red dot appear on his cheek, and found her heart beating a little more quickly. Perhaps there was more emotion within him than she had expected – more than *he* had ever expected also it seemed, given his response! "You may think me hasty in speaking so, but I assure you, it comes from my heart." Coughing, Lord Alderton kept his gaze turned away. "If you will allow me a little time, Lady Cassandra, then I might be able to consider exactly what it is that currently resides within me when it comes to you. I have never permitted myself to think on it before, dismissing it without even the smallest consideration." His eyes darted to hers for a moment as he lifted one shoulder. "As I have said, I am always a gentleman who is focused on practicality. I have never needed to consider such things before."

"I understand."

His smile lifted the edges of his mouth, stealing some of the seriousness from his expression.

"I hope that I will be able to respond to you in the way that you desire. I just require some time to consider things."

A weight began to lift from her shoulders but, as they began to walk beside each other again, Cassandra tilted her head, slowing her steps to consider him and what he had said. Was he genuine in what he had told her? It had come rather quickly, she supposed, but his explanation had been fair. Thus far, he seemed to have proven himself entirely. There was nothing in his character which Lady Yardley or Lord Sherbourne had found to complain of and thereafter, what had been placed in 'The London Ledger', had, it seemed, encouraged him to prove himself to her, had it not? Surely now she could allow him a little time to consider his own heart, particularly when he had never permitted himself to think on it before.

"If it is of any benefit to you to hear this, I am sure that my heart will respond rather quickly to your encouragements." Finally, Lord Alderton looked at her, although his gaze did not linger, his cheeks now flushing scarlet. "Forgive me, Lady Cassandra, I am discomforting myself. I am not the sort of fellow inclined to speak so openly."

"I am all the more grateful to you for being so open with me." Taking a deep breath, she found herself smiling, a good deal more at ease than she had been only some moments ago. "Certainly, I can give you some time to consider all that you must. How glad I am to have found the courage to speak with you about my own heart."

Lord Alderton laughed.

"As am I," he admitted. "For had you not had such courage, then I fear that our acquaintance might have come to an end, and such a thing would have devastated me, I believe." He leaned towards her, his mouth close to her ear as their steps slowed all the more. "And I would not wish to ever be apart from you."

Much to her astonishment, his nearness did not bring Cassandra even a flicker of feeling. Her skin did not prickle, goosebumps did not break out across it, and she did not giggle lightly. No fire of delight began to smolder within her, her heart did not pound and, all in all, it was as though a simple friend had spoken to her rather than a gentleman with whom she might find herself in love. Forcing a smile, she quickly turned her head away and fixed her gaze straight ahead, now concerned by her lack of feeling. She had told herself that, *if* Lord Alderton declared that yes, he could find himself in love with her, she would then be able to set her heart free. Except now, she felt nothing in response. She had expected a powerful emotion to overwhelm her, so that all she wanted to do was be swept up into his arms – but it did not come. In fact, the only time she had ever felt that way was when she had been dancing with Lord Sherbourne.

Her heart turned over in her chest.

"Look." Lord Alderton's tone had dropped somewhat as Cassandra attempted to steady herself, suddenly feeling all of a tremble. "Is that not Lord Sherbourne?" It was as though fate was placing him directly before her gaze, showing her how her heart was now pounding as she caught sight of him. A desire immediately began to blossom, growing steadily as they drew closer – a desire to drop Lord Alderton's arm, to run to Lord Sherbourne, and to tell him what she had just discovered about her heart. It was as if she was back in the ballroom on the evening when they had waltzed, recalling how strong his arm had been around her waist, how tightly his hand had clasped hers – and how much she wanted to have him close to her again. "I do not think that we should draw near." Lord Alderton huffed out a long breath. "And I do hope that you have reconsidered your close acquaintance with Lord Sherbourne, and that Lady Yardley has done the same."

Despite believing that Lord Alderton was doing his best to protect her, a jarring anger shot through Cassandra and she stiffened instantly, lifting her head.

"Nothing has been proven as yet."

Her quick response and hard gaze met Lord Alderton's eyes as his eyebrows lifted in obvious surprise.

"You are still determined to cling to him then."

Cassandra shook her head, managing to keep her tone measured.

"I am determined to be fair, Lord Alderton."

Gone was the pleasantness between them, the softness of her voice and the gentleness of his. Instead, their voices were heavier now, with dark expressions flickering across both faces.

"I wish you would listen to me." Lord Alderton sighed heavily, his displeasure obvious. "Lord Sherbourne is not the gentleman he purports to be."

Cassandra withdrew her hand from his arm, unwilling to stand close to Lord Alderton any longer. She disliked his determination to prove that Lord Sherbourne was a gentleman who pretended to be something he was not, and was all the more displeased that he would expect her to agree with him wholeheartedly – especially when the accusation was nothing more than a rumor as yet.

"I shall go to speak with him."

Her chin lifted, a challenge sparking in her eyes, and Lord Alderton shook his head.

"I shall not, but I will remain here to wait for your return, Lady Cassandra."

She held his gaze steadily.

"As you wish, Lord Alderton."

Lady Yardley said nothing to the gentleman as he strode past to wait a short distance away and, with a wave of her hand, encouraged Cassandra forward. She went at once, speaking Lord Sherbourne's name and seeing how he started, clearly having been unaware of her presence beforehand.

"Good afternoon, Lady Cassandra." His jaw jutted forward a little, his brows low and heavy over his eyes. "Is that Lord Alderton I see waiting for you?"

Cassandra nodded.

"It is."

Lord Sherbourne sighed, but said nothing more, leaving

Cassandra in something of a quandary. Should she speak of the diamond bracelet or should she remain silent? To her eyes, Lord Sherbourne was not in his usual state of mind. He was always smiling, amiable, and eager for conversation, but now this dull, crumpled creature was nothing like the gentleman she knew so well.

"I have been waiting for your visit." Speaking softly, Cassandra tried to smile, but Lord Sherbourne refused to meet her gaze. "At the very least I thought you would have sent a note."

"A note about...?"

A little astonished, it took her a moment to respond.

"A note about what Lord Alderton has laid at your feet, of course."

Finally, Lord Sherbourne turned his head a little so that their eyes met.

"I thought you believed me, Cassandra." His voice was low, his eyes dull. "I thought you believed that I was not a thief."

"Yes, yes, I do." Urgent in her determination for him to believe her, Cassandra stepped forward, one hand going out to his, only for Lord Sherbourne immediately to fold his arms over his chest so that she could not reach him. Her heart twisted. "Do you not think it wise to give us an explanation? We are your friends, are we not? Why would you not want to tell us what has happened?"

Lord Sherbourne sighed heavily, his hands dropping to his sides.

"What difference would it make?"

Cassandra reached for his hand for the second time, managing to latch her fingers around his wrist.

"I do not understand."

Lord Sherbourne's eyes went to Lord Alderton.

"Do not permit me to interrupt your time with Lord Alderton, Lady Cassandra. I am sure that your time with him will be most enjoyable."

Cassandra swallowed hard, her throat constricting as tears began to burn in her eyes. She did not know what Lord Sherbourne was doing, other than realizing that he was attempting to push her away, towards Lord Alderton. How could he have changed so suddenly? And what were his reasons for doing so?

"Would you not join us?"

It was a foolish question, she knew, for Lord Sherbourne's jaw immediately tightened and his eyes flashed.

"I should not like to be anywhere near Lord Alderton at present." The darkness of his voice struck at Cassandra's heart. "Forgive me, Lady Cassandra. I must bid you good afternoon for the moment."

Finding the same courage which had been there when she had spoken truthfully to Lord Alderton, Cassandra did not release his wrist but instead stepped forward.

"Promise me that you will come to speak with me soon."

Lord Sherbourne's eyes flared as he looked toward her. Cassandra let her hand drift to his fingers, keeping it hidden from Lord Alderton and Lady Yardley's view. Her fingers found his, wrapping gently around them, and after a few moments, Lord Sherbourne finally squeezed them back.

"I do not know what you want from me."

Cassandra could not answer his question. The truth was, she was not certain what she wanted from Lord Sherbourne either, but the thought of this being their acquaintance, this strange confusing, awkward connection, was not something she could accept.

"I want to understand. I do not know why you have this diamond bracelet, but even if the rumors begin to circulate through society, I shall be found standing by your side, trusting you and your word." Trying to encourage him, she smiled into his eyes. "I still need your advice and your guidance when it comes to the gentlemen of the *ton* and pray, do not think that I am settled on Lord Alderton, for I assure you that I am not. Do not give in to fear, Lord Sherbourne, and please do not step away from me. I do not think that I could bear it."

It was only as she spoke those words that Cassandra released the depths of pain she would sink to, should she be set apart from Lord Sherbourne for the remainder of the Season. The gentleman held her gaze for some minutes and after a few seconds, let out a heavy breath, dropped his head forward, and allowed his fingers to rub gently across the back of her hand.

"Go to Lord Alderton, Lady Cassandra." His shoulders stooped low as if weighted and Cassandra's eyes flooded with sharp, unexpected tears. "If I do decide an explanation for what has happened is worthwhile, I shall inform you of it, of course. But for the moment, I find myself filled with very little hope."

"Then allow me to help you," Cassandra begged, still a little uncertain as to what he meant, only for Lord Sherbourne to shake his head. Without another word, he released her hand and gestured for her to go to Lord Alderton once more. With tears still burning in the corners of her eyes, Cassandra found herself turning away from him and instead, her steps going towards the gentleman she did not want to be in company with. Her heart seemed to stay behind her, close to Lord Sherbourne, and the further away she went from him, the more it began to break.

CHAPTER THIRTEEN

"*A*nd did you say that your father would be abroad for some time?" Cassandra only nodded as she and Lord Alderton made their way around London. This was the second time in some four days that he had called on her and this time, they were taking a ride in his phaeton. Lord Sherbourne still had not come to call, and Cassandra's feelings were still very much confused. "You have very little knowledge as to when he will return?"

Cassandra looked up at him, her frustration firing a sudden boldness within her, for he was asking the same questions about her father as he had done before, without any real explanation as to why.

"As I have said before, Lord Alderton, I have very little knowledge of my father's plans. I am to stay with Lady Yardley for as long as it is required, even when the Season ends." She took a breath. "Is there a reason that you have asked me these things when my father has already been the topic of our discussions once before?

Lord Alderton flushed a little and turned his gaze away from her.

"Forgive me my persistent questions. They are well meant."

"In what way?"

Again, Cassandra did not hold herself back, asking questions that Lord Alderton could not simply ignore. Lord Alderton smiled and touched her hand lightly for a moment before taking the reins again.

"I ask it because I must consider my future," he told her, his voice rather loud over the din of the phaeton wheels on the cobbled streets. "And if someone's father is on the continent, then I will not be able to ask him directly whether or not I might pursue his daughter."

At this, Cassandra caught her breath, her frustrations flooding away. In only a matter of days, Lord Alderton had gone from speaking of them both as a practical match and now, here he was speaking about going to her father. Had there been some great change within his own heart? Had he only just realized the depths of his affection? He had not used words of love as yet, but perhaps it was simply because he had not the words for it, given how unused to it he was.

"You appear a little surprised." Lord Alderton chuckled. "I will not hold that against you. It is mayhap a little sudden, but we have spent a great deal of time together these last few weeks." His smile dipped. "I confess to you, my feelings – now unguarded and no longer hidden – are a good deal more than I ever expected."

No thrill of excitement nor happiness warmed Cassandra's heart. She was not overcome by a sudden joy, she did not want to clap her hands and cry aloud for the sheer relief of it. She had opened her heart to him, yes, but now it seemed that her heart was not responding to his words in any way. Cassandra bit her lip, her brow furrowing. She had silently believed that, once words of affection were spoken, she would fall in love easily with Lord Alderton - except now, she realized, she felt nothing in particular at all.

"You have said nothing these last few minutes." Lord Alderton touched her hand for the second time, but no jolt of feeling ran through her. "I had hoped it would bring you a little joy to hear such a declaration."

"Of course it does." Murmuring softly, Cassandra fought to bring any sense of happiness to her expression. "It is a little surprising, as you have said."

As she spoke, Cassandra felt invisible chains slip themselves around her wrist, tying her to Lord Alderton. She had been the one who had spoken of love, had told him how much she sought a love match and now he was declaring his feelings for her, she felt nothing in response. But if she had asked for such a thing, if she had expected to fall in love with him, could she really reject him now? To do so would be shameful, would it not, not after everything he now offered her?

"I must also apologize for the trials I have brought you as regards Lord Sherbourne," Lord Alderton continued, fiercely striking a stake through her already pained heart simply by mentioning his name. "I can imagine it would have been very difficult indeed to hear such things, given that he is so closely acquainted with you."

"He is my friend." Cassandra spoke without thinking, seeing how he frowned, eyes flaring. "I still consider him as such."

"Even though you know he has stolen a diamond bracelet?"

Gritting her teeth for a moment, Cassandra turned her head away. Lord Sherbourne had not given her an explanation as yet, and certainly did not seem to want to, either, given both his absence and his silence. In fact, did it not appear as though he was deliberately separating himself from her? The pain from thinking such a thing sent a fresh wave of agony through her, to the point that Cassandra was forced to bend forward a little, one hand pressed lightly against her heart.

"Such things do not matter, I suppose," Lord Alderton continued with a shrug. "Once we are courting, your acquaintance with the gentleman need not continue." A fierce indignation took hold of her, and a sharp response sprang to her lips, but she turned her head away instead, holding the words back. Resentment and exasperation rolled together into a heavy ball, settling into the pit of her stomach. How dare he tell her whom she could keep as an acquaintance? This could not be genuine affection, for surely a gentleman did not seek to control his lady, did not require that she do as he demanded, nor expect her to take on his opinions as her own? And yet, in stating such a thing as that, was it not precisely what Lord Alderton expected of her? "Alas, our time is at an end and I suppose I must now return you to Lady Yardley."

Lord Alderton did not appear to notice how little she'd spoken and, with relief, Cassandra looked to the footman who drew near, ready to help her down from the phaeton, one hand outstretched. Both her mind and her heart were pushing her from Lord Alderton's company, urging her away from him as fast as she could go. When her feet touched the ground, it was as though they wanted her to fly from him and into the townhouse, and it was only when she rolled her hands into fists and forced in slow breaths, that she was able to remain exactly where she stood. Lord Alderton had also jumped down from the phaeton, coming around to stand next to her. He reached for her hand, but Cassandra did not give it.

"A very pleasant ride, was it not?" His hand remained stretched out towards her, as he looked at her with one brow slightly lifted. Feeling more than awkward, Cassandra eventually relented and accepted his hand. When he bowed over it, his lips brushing the back of her hand, she did nothing but shudder. Evidently mistaking this for a thrill of delight, Lord Alderton grinned, his eyes dancing.

"I am glad to see that you feel much the same as I." Murmuring a little more quietly, he took a step closer to her, clutching at her hand still. "I believe I shall write to your father soon, Lady Cassandra. My feelings are growing with such significance, I do not think that it would be prudent to wait much longer."

A furious hopelessness filled her heart. This is what she had told him she wanted, but now it was being offered to her, her heart was tugging *away* from him... and towards someone else.

Cassandra swallowed at the lump forming in her throat. She had never once expected to find that the gentleman who claimed to be in love with her was not someone whom she herself desired! Nor, she considered, as Lord Alderton continued to speak of his intentions, had she expected to find her thoughts going to a gentleman who had made no efforts whatsoever to capture her heart.

What would Lord Sherbourne's expression be, should she tell him that she was now being courted by Lord Alderton? Would he be pleased? Or would there be something more there?

Lord Alderton's voice became nothing more than a whine, his presence a mere shadow. Her heart began to ache terribly as her thoughts lingered on Lord Sherbourne. *He* was the one her thoughts had so often turned to, *he* was the one she had found herself thinking of over and over again. When they had danced the waltz, his nearness had been something she could not escape from and, Cassandra realized, something she had continually desired to return to. If Lord Sherbourne gave her even the smallest encouragement, Cassandra recognized just how quickly she would press herself into his arms.

I do not want to be courted by Lord Alderton. I want... I want Lord Sherbourne.

Her breath hitched, her feet turning her away from Lord Alderton, before he had even finished speaking. Suddenly, the only thing she desired was to be in Lord Sherbourne's company so that she might look into her heart and see precisely what it was that blossomed there – but first, she would have to speak to her cousin. She would have to tell her about Lord Alderton, and beg for her advice as to what she ought to do next.

Hurrying inside – and leaving a somewhat bemused Lord Alderton behind – Cassandra practically threw her gloves and bonnet at the butler before hurrying to the drawing room, expecting Lady Yardley to be there. Her eyes closed, her heart hammering as the vacant room greeted her. Her thoughts were in turmoil, the truth of her heart finally revealing itself to her. Now, she realized, she cared *only* for Lord Sherbourne. Her heart was filled with an affection for *him* and not for Lord Alderton. Did she have any hope that her affection would be returned? Or was she find to herself in a dark pit, lost in confusion and sorrow?

Her eyes opened, her breathing steadying as she recalled just how many times they had shared a gentle smile or a soft touch. Could it be that Lord Sherbourne had some affection for her but had hidden it – even from himself – in much the way that Lord Alderton had done? Could she allow herself a flickering hope?

The door opened and she turned swiftly, her eyes flaring wide at the sight of the very gentleman of whom she had been thinking. Whether it was boldness or fear about the situation with Lord Alderton, she did not know, but something pushed her forward and, in only a moment, Cassandra found herself clasped in his arms.

~

"I MUST SPEAK WITH YOU."

Lord Knoxbridge swirled his whisky around his glass.

"Then speak," he replied mildly, smiling back at Jonathan from where he sat. "And please sit down, your constant pacing is making me feel rather fatigued."

Jonathan dropped into a chair but did not smile.

"I want to know who you told about the bracelet." He came to the point directly, so that no time would be wasted, his jaw tight, and anger beginning to bubble in the pit of his stomach. "I know you must have said something."

Lord Knoxbridge's smile shattered.

"I have said nothing." Taking a sip of his whisky, he waved one hand. "I know you may think me a little foolish, but I assure you that I have said nothing about the diamond bracelet to anyone. I have kept that information to myself, I promise you." The anger which had burned so fiercely through Jonathan instantly began to dissipate as Lord Knoxbridge tilted his head, one eyebrow lifted. "I did not tell a soul." Sitting back in his chair, appearing not in any way disconcerted, Lord Knoxbridge's tone remained mild. "I can, when I wish to, keep certain secrets."

"You did not tell anyone about the bracelet?" Jonathan leaned forward, fixing Lord Knoxbridge with his gaze. "Not even one single person?"

Lord Knoxbridge shook his head.

"I can promise you that I have said not one single word." Jonathan sat back in his chair, suddenly all the more confused. He had been quite sure that Lord Knoxbridge was the reason for Lord Alderton's accusation but now, it appeared that he had been entirely mistaken. "I think you should explain to me what has happened." Snapping his fingers so the footman would bring them both something to drink, Lord Knoxbridge settled his gaze back upon Jonathan. "Something has happened with regard to this bracelet?"

"Yes." Somewhat relieved that his friend had not reacted badly to his sharpness, Jonathan let out a slow breath. "Lord Alderton accused me of stealing the bracelet – and said so in front of Lady Yardley and Lady Cassandra. I do not know how he came to know about it."

"And therefore, you believed I was the one who had told him."

Guilt searing him, Jonathan nodded, ducking his head.

"Forgive me, it was a little unfair of me to rush to that conclusion, but given that you are the only one I had talked to, I–"

"I do not blame you." Lord Knoxbridge waved one hand. "No, no, for I am quite untrustworthy." He shrugged both shoulders. "It is understandable for you to think that I was the one to blame." Pausing for a moment to take the drinks from the footman, Lord Knoxbridge waited until the man had taken his leave before he continued. "And you say that Lord Alderton threw this at you in the presence of Lady Cassandra?"

Nodding, Jonathan winced as he recalled the conversation.

"I think that he is doing his best to protect her, having

heard these rumors. He fears, mayhap, that I would be an unsuitable acquaintance, should those rumors come to light." Shaking his head, he ran one hand through his hair, letting out a heavy sigh. "I am very relieved to know that, as yet, these whispers have not become known throughout society."

Lord Knoxbridge frowned, running one hand over his chin before bringing his glass to his lips. Swallowing, he then leaned forward, his expression serious.

"There is also one other reason why the gentleman might have stated such a thing." One finger pointed out in Jonathan's direction but, a little confused, Jonathan waited for his friend to continue. Lord Knoxbridge arched an eyebrow, but silence was his only response – meaning that he threw his hand up, let out a loud exclamation, and then threw himself back in his chair. "*Please* do not tell me that you have not considered the fact that Lord Alderton might be doing his very best to break the bond between yourself and Lady Cassandra?"

Jonathan made to laugh, only for the sound to stick in his throat, his smile crumpling. This was something that he had never thought about before.

"But why would he do so? He knows very well that I am here only to aid Lady Yardley and Lady Cassandra."

"Precisely."

Confused, Jonathan spread out both hands, one still clutching at his glass.

"What does that mean?"

Lord Knoxbridge sighed and rolled his eyes, clearly exasperated.

"There is a chance that Lord Alderton is aware that there is something unscrupulous about himself – something he does not wish you or Lady Cassandra to find out – so therefore, he is making certain that you are vilified in her eyes, so you pose no threat."

"To do so would take a great deal of planning." Still finding it a little unbelievable, Jonathan shook his head. "And he would also have had to find out about the bracelet in some way."

"Unless, of course, he was the one who was instrumental in it ending up in your pocket."

Taking a breath, Jonathan said nothing, letting his friend's words run around his mind. If he were to accept such a thing as true, then it would mean that Lord Alderton was not the gentleman he appeared to be. Frowning, he recalled stepping from White's on the evening he had discovered the bracelet, bumping into various gentlemen as he stumbled from the establishment – but he could not recall seeing Lord Alderton's face. But, then again, he could not remember very much about that evening at all. Was there a chance that Lord Alderton had done such a thing?

"It cannot be so." Shaking his head, he threw up both hands. "There is nothing about his character which I have found to be of defect. There is nothing which would make him at all unsuitable... as far as I have discovered."

"It does not mean that my suggestion is incorrect." Lord Knoxbridge frowned. "Should I wish it, I am quite certain that I would be able to hide everything I have done from society's eyes. I could make the pretense that I was entirely proper in all things. Lord Alderton could very easily have something that he is attempting to hide."

In considering this, Jonathan felt his mind heavily burdened. He had always disliked Lord Alderton but had told himself that it was simply because of how close he was becoming with Lady Cassandra. Fighting against his feelings, he had also fought against any consideration that Lord Alderton might not be as he appeared.

"There is another thing in what I am suggesting," Lord Knoxbridge continued quietly. "Lord Alderton might very well be a gentleman by appearance but still carry malevolence in his heart – and if he desires Lady Cassandra for himself, for whatever reason, he might have seen in you what *I* have witnessed also... and want to put an end to it."

Jonathan swallowed hard and took a sip from his glass rather than respond. There was something in what Lord Knoxbridge was suggesting, something he had never allowed himself to think on. He had always assumed that Lord Alderton had been trying to protect Lady Cassandra, but what if his assumptions had been wrong? What if there was something darker there, something which might pull Lady Cassandra into a depth of shadow should her close connection to Lord Alderton continue?

A long breath escaped him as he rubbed one hand over his face.

"What am I to do?"

Lord Knoxbridge let out a snort.

"Must I truly aid you in this also?" Taking Jonathan's silence as proof of this, he waved one hand in a furious fashion. "You are friends with Lady Yardley, are you not?" The short, sharp words evidenced his frustration that Jonathan had not thought of this resolution himself. "Why do you not consider using 'The London Ledger'?"

"In what way?"

"First of all, in attempting to find the owner of the diamond bracelet." Lord Knoxbridge finished his whisky, set the glass on the table beside him, then leaned forward with his elbows on his knees and fixed Jonathan with a hard gaze. "I do not know why we have not thought of this before. You should use 'The London Ledger' to state that this bracelet has been discovered and that you seek the rightful owner. I am sure that you will be able to use the Ledger to find the truth about Lord Alderton's motivations also." Chuckling quietly, Lord Knoxbridge shook his head. "Though do not ask me what it is you should do in *that* regard, for I have no particular idea. But the Ledger has proven useful and I am sure it will do so again."

Taking a deeper breath, Jonathan pushed himself to his feet, a determination beginning to flood him.

"Yes, you are right – although if I state that I have the bracelet, then Lord Alderton will be able to say it is because I am a thief and I have only decided to return it because I was discovered."

"Or you could ask Lady Cassandra to put her name to it." With a shake of his head, Lord Knoxbridge smiled. "If you wish for my advice, Sherbourne, it is to tell Cassandra the truth. Tell her everything, and I am sure that she will be more than willing to put her name to such a statement. That way, no one will be able to claim that *she* is a thief – least of all, Lord Alderton." The idea was a wise one, but the thought of speaking so openly to Lady Cassandra sent a spiral of worry into Jonathan's heart. No doubt, in speaking of that, it would then lead to him telling her the truth about his own feelings. "And pray do not look so afraid about what you must tell her." Lord Knoxbridge chuckled, gesturing to the footman with one hand for another whisky and with the other, waving Jonathan away. "To see you struggle with your feelings for Lady Cassandra has been most tiresome, so I am hopeful that this will bring it to an end."

Snorting, Jonathan shot his friend a wry smile.

"Thank you, Knoxbridge. You have been very helpful".

"But of course." Sitting back in his chair, Lord

Knoxbridge grinned. "You do not realize how glad I am to know that *I* shall never find myself in such difficulty over a young lady."

"I would not be certain of that."

Jonathan chuckled at Lord Knoxbridge's shudder, waved a hand, and then walked from White's, filled with a strengthening determination as he turned himself in the direction of Lady Yardley's townhouse.

CHAPTER FOURTEEN

*W*alking directly into the drawing room, his heart pounding as he thought about what he wanted to say to Lady Cassandra, Jonathan was suddenly accosted by a tumble of arms and legs. The arms clasped themselves around him so tightly that for a moment, he could not breathe. It was only after a few moments that he realized it was none other than Lady Cassandra who held him so.

"Lady Cassandra?" Her head rested on his shoulder, his arms finding her waist so they might slip around her. They stood close together and, as Jonathan dropped his head a little, the desire to press his lips to hers was so strong that it took all of his inner strength not to do so. "Is something wrong?"

Immediately her frame began to shake, and Jonathan tugged her a little closer, his concern growing.

"I was with Lord Alderton." Her head lifted a little from his shoulder, her eyes shimmering gently as she gazed into his. "He took me for a ride in his phaeton and I–"

Immediately, Jonathan's eyes flared, a tight hand grasping his heart.

"I pray he did nothing to injure you?"

"No, he did not."

Lady Cassandra's gaze dropped to his mouth and Jonathan sucked in air. Could it be that she was battling the very same thoughts as he? Grimacing slightly at his selfish thought, Jonathan reminded himself that Lady Cassandra was somewhat upset, and allowing himself to linger on thoughts of kissing her was most inappropriate.

"Then what is the matter? Why do you appear so upset?"

To his utter astonishment, Lady Cassandra leaned back and brushed the back of her fingers lightly across his cheek. A single tear fell from her eyes but her smile was present still.

"I am not upset out of sorrow, but rather from realizing something significant." Her soft voice was a melody, seizing his worries and instead, replacing them with joy before he even knew why. "Lord Alderton declared that he has some feelings for me, some affection, and that he intends to write to my father."

His joy crumpled in on itself, his smile faltering.

"Oh." Was this what she had wanted to speak with him about? Did she think he wished to know of her success? "That is... That is excellent."

Lady Cassandra shook her head, another tear dropping onto her cheek, whirling up his confusion once again.

"No, that is not what I meant. When Lord Alderton told me of his feelings, I confess that it did not-"

"Cassandra!" The door behind them was flung open and suddenly, Lady Yardley charged through it, coming straight towards her cousin, her hands outstretched. Lady

Cassandra herself stepped back as Jonathan's hands fell to his sides, his frustration abounding that yet again, he had been interrupted. "The butler told me that you came into the house all of a tizzy," Lady Yardley exclaimed, grasping Lady Cassandra's hands. "What happened?"

"I was just about to explain the same to Lord Sherbourne." Lady Cassandra gestured to a chair. "Perhaps we might sit?"

"And if I might join you?" Jonathan managed a brief smile as both ladies looked at him. "There is something important I wish to share with you both, also. Something which requires your aid, Lady Cassandra, and something, I am afraid, which casts doubt upon Lord Alderton."

He looked steadily at Lady Cassandra, expecting to see her eyes flare with worry but, instead, she just merely nodded and shrugged one shoulder. She did not seem in any way concerned about what he might say of Lord Alderton. Could it be that the feelings she'd thought she possessed were no longer at the fore?

"Then who shall begin?"

Lady Yardley looked from one to the other and Jonathan, even though he knew it was not quite proper to demand that he go first, gestured to Lady Cassandra as they all sat down.

"If I might?" He dropped his hand. "I think that what I might have to say could influence what you say in return."

Lady Cassandra hesitated but then nodded.

"Certainly."

Keeping her hands folded in her lap, she waited for him to speak and, after a moment or two, Jonathan began.

"First, I must state that I do have a diamond bracelet in my possession – a bracelet which mysteriously appeared in my coat pocket after I had spent some time at White's. Its existence there utterly puzzled me, and at the time I discussed it with Lord Knoxbridge, attempting to work out how best to determine who owned it. I had achieved no success in that search when Lord Alderton delivered his accusations. I have just now come from speaking with Lord Knoxbridge again, about this matter. As frustrating as it is, he appears to have spoken a good deal more sense than I had ever thought possible." This brought with it a wry smile from Lady Cassandra and a chuckle from Lady Yardley, but Jonathan kept his expression serious. "I am not pretending that this is an entirely correct scenario. I may have misjudged the gentleman, and all of this may be nothing more than a foolish suggestion on our part, but Lord Knoxbridge made the suggestion that the diamond bracelet and Lord Alderton's accusations, delivered specifically to you, were linked."

At this, Lady Cassandra caught her breath.

"I do not understand what you mean."

Jonathan spread his hands, a little concerned that the heaviness on Lady Cassandra's face was an indication that she would not accept his explanation. Had he been mistaken in thinking that she cared very little for Lord Alderton? Perhaps she cared about him now, as much as ever.

"Lord Knoxbridge questioned how Lord Alderton had known of this diamond bracelet, given that he had heard no rumors, and why Lord Alderton would not state the name of the lady to whom the bracelet belonged." Licking his lips, relief flooded him as Lady Yardley began to nod. "It was suggested that Lord Alderton has deliberately created a situation so that I could be decried as a thief at a time of his choosing – at a time when it was most required. When it was best for him."

Lady Cassandra did not smile nor nod, however. Instead, a light frown continued to grow across her forehead.

"What is it that you are suggesting?"

"What if the reason Lord Alderton knew of the diamond bracelet in my possession was that he was the one who put it there? What if there are no rumors?" Jonathan asked, sweat breaking out across his forehead as he fought to explain himself.

"If he had done so, it would mean that he did it purpose-fully." Lady Cassandra passed one hand over her forehead, her frown cutting a line between her brows. "You believe that he *deliberately* set the diamond bracelet into your pocket, so that, should he need to, he could accuse you of thievery?" Her hands flung upwards for a moment. "I cannot see a reason why he would act in such a way."

"Because he wanted to make certain that you did not become too close to Lady Cassandra." Lady Yardley spoke quietly, directing her words to Jonathan, who nodded, drop-ping his gaze away from Lady Cassandra, heat spiraling upwards within him. "Clearly he has seen your reactions, as I have also, and thus, you believe that he is doing what he can to make certain that you do not attempt to take the lady away from his side."

Jonathan's heart leaped up into his throat and he dared not look at Lady Cassandra. He had not yet had time to talk to her about his feelings and, with all of the confusion, had not even attempted to consider their true depth – but Lady Yardley had obviously seen them well before he had found them within his heart.

"It seems as though I have been blind." Still refusing to look at Lady Cassandra, Jonathan fixed his gaze on Lady Yardley. "I found myself disliking Lord Alderton. I have never had any particular reason for why, however, given that his character did not appear to have any defect, and that what we put in the Ledger did not bring any difficulty, but rather clarity for Lady Cassandra." Pausing, he shook his head, a small sigh escaping from him. "Lord Knoxbridge, however, reminded me that there is often more to a gentleman's character than he is willing to reveal, suggesting that there is most likely something about Lord Alderton that he does not want us to know. Perhaps he does seek to push me away from Cassandra. If he fears that I might become more dear to her than he is, then by this use of the bracelet, he would have some way of proving to her that I am not the gentleman I seem to be. That I am a thief, a scoundrel. Whatever I might say about him, he will be able to say worse of me, and therefore will push Lady Cassandra as far from me as he can."

Fully aware of just how hot his face was, he stopped abruptly and dropped his head low, taking in a long breath in the hope of pushing some of the warmth away.

"Cassandra?" Lady Yardley spoke softly. "What do you think of this?"

When Jonathan finally dared to glance at her, the young lady's cheeks were rather pink, but her eyes were dazzling, fastening to his, refusing to look anywhere but him. She took some moments to reply, but there was, Jonathan noted, no immediate refusal to believe what he had said.

"I am astonished to hear the suggestion, but I do not think I should dismiss it."

"It does seem rather determined." Lady Yardley said, rubbing one hand over her eyes, her lips tugging to one side of her face. "If it is true, then Lord Alderton appears singular in his determination to garner Cassandra's approval – which does not suggest that he truly cares for you, my dear." Speaking now to Lady Cassandra, Lady Yardley sighed softly. "I do not say so to upset you, but rather because I do not see affection within Lord Alderton's conduct. A gentleman does not behave in an underhanded manner simply to force a lady into his affections. It seems to me that there is a significant possibility that Lord Alderton has ulterior motives. If he truly cares for you, then he would allow you to make your own choice."

Much to Jonathan's relief, Lady Cassandra nodded, but there came no sudden tears in her eyes, no hand flying to her mouth, no quick gasp of breath. All in all, she appeared quite calm.

"I confess I have found much the same." Sitting forward in her chair, Lady Cassandra clasped her hands together. "This is what I wanted to tell you, Norah. When I came back from my phaeton ride with Lord Alderton, I found myself in such a state of confusion, it was all I could do not to run into the house to get away from him."

"Goodness." Lady Yardley's eyes flared. "Whatever did he say to make you feel so?"

Lady Cassandra sat back, her lip caught between her teeth as she considered her reply.

"He told me that I would not be permitted to continue my acquaintance with Lord Sherbourne once we were courting." Gentle eyes turned to his and Jonathan was cocooned by both a sense of relief and a thread of anger over Lord Alderton's demands. "I did not think that a gentleman who claimed to care for me would demand obedience in such a way. I did not like the fact that he was so sure of your guilt that he decreed that I believe it too, once we were courting. I do not think it is fair for a man to make such demands."

"Most would agree with you," Lady Yardley murmured, but Lady Cassandra barely gave her a glance.

"And with all of this," Lady Cassandra continued, her brows lowering, her words coming a little more slowly now, "I find myself somewhat perturbed that he has often asked me about my father and his travels."

An idle thought began to force its way into Jonathan's mind.

"And how did he seem when you told him that your father would be on the continent for some time?"

Lady Cassandra considered, her eyes lingering on his.

"If I am to be truthful, I would say that he did not show any frustration over that fact. Now that I think of it, I did catch him smiling."

The same thought swirling around Jonathan's mind appeared to have made its way into Lady Yardley's mind also, for she scowled darkly, her eyes holding a spark of fire.

"Might I ask, Cassandra, if Lord Alderton was present when Lord Darlington asked openly about your dowry?"

Jonathan held his breath, his gaze swiveling back towards Lady Cassandra, with Lady Yardley's question hanging in the air. Color slowly began to fade from Lady Cassandra's cheeks. She blinked rapidly, then squeezed her eyes tight shut.

"I do recall that he overheard him, yes. He made an exclamation of disapproval."

"Then," Lady Yardley murmured quietly, "there is a chance that Lord Alderton is eager for your dowry. Do you believe his words of affection?"

Lady Cassandra's eyes opened, but rather than looking at her cousin, she turned to Jonathan.

"When I was in the phaeton, I was torn with guilt. I always believed that I would fall quickly in love with a gentleman who declared himself fond of me. However, it seems that my feelings do *not* return Lord Alderton's words of affection. If I am to be truthful, they direct themselves in an entirely different direction."

Jonathan was the one to catch his breath, hoping beyond hope that what she had said meant precisely what he so eagerly desired.

"Very well." Lady Yardley's voice was quiet, the seriousness of their current situation spreading through the room. "Lord Sherbourne, you say that you only have suspicions at this point. I feel that we must prove this, for Cassandra's sake."

"As do I," Jonathan replied firmly. "I must know whether or not he placed this diamond bracelet in my pocket, and I must find the true owner of it. Therefore, I wondered if I might use 'The London Ledger' to place a small advertisement stating that a diamond bracelet has been found." His head turned, and he looked at Lady Yardley, seeing her eyebrows lift. "I am afraid that if I say that I have it, Lord Alderton will be able to use that as leverage to throw me from society. I do not think that he cares how much I am damaged by what he says. He only wants me away from Lady Cassandra and, I fear, will go to any lengths to achieve that."

"You may say that I have found it." Lady Cassandra's voice was warm and filled with a gentleness which made Jonathan smile with relief. "We could not have the *ton* thinking such things of you. And while you are writing that, cousin, I have something else which I think I should like you to put in."

"What is it?"

She smiled.

"I have a plan to force the truth from Lord Alderton's

lips. I wish to do so not only for myself but also for the other young ladies of the *ton*. They must also know of his true character, must they not?"

Jonathan looked at Lady Cassandra for a long moment as she smiled at her cousin, seeing the gentle glow in her eyes, the soft smile on her lips, and the flush which filled her cheeks. Whatever it was that she intended, it was clear now that she found relief in being able to separate herself from Lord Alderton - and that made his own heart sing with a furious hope – a hope, he prayed, which would not remain unfulfilled for too much longer.

CHAPTER FIFTEEN

"Good evening, Lord Alderton."

How much easier it was for her to smile, now that she knew what plan was to be unfolded this evening!

"Good evening, Lady Cassandra." Lord Alderton smiled, bowed, then took her hand in his. "I am so very glad to see you here this evening. Perhaps we shall have our waltz! You are aware that I am still waiting for that wonderous moment to take place?"

"How is it that in all of our time together, we have not yet managed to waltz?" She tipped her head and let a delicate smile touch her lips. "It seems as though fate is preventing us from standing up together."

Lord Alderton chuckled.

"Fate be damned, I have made my intentions quite clear, I think, and now intend to write to your father very soon. I will be sorry if he cannot return in time for our betrothal but –"

"Come now, you must sign my dance card before we lose any further time."

Choosing to ignore Lord Alderton's talk of betrothal, Cassandra gave him a quick smile and slipped the dance card from her wrist. She had no intention of standing up with him for the waltz, but by that time of the evening, she was convinced that all would be at an end between them.

"Very well, very well." Lord Alderton chuckled as he took the dance card from her fingers. "It seems that this is to be the very best of evenings!"

A small, twisted smile crossed Cassandra's lips, but she dropped her head, taking the dance card from him and placing it back upon her wrist, allowing that action to hide her face from his eyes. What she need *not* do was give herself away! It was with relief that she considered what would soon take place, for this evening would prove to her, once and for all, that Lord Alderton was not as he seemed, although he had attempted to cloak himself with a shroud of affection and geniality. If there was more to his character, then there was more to his attachment to her than there appeared.

"In speaking of betrothal, it occurs to me that you have not often spoken of your estate." She smiled at him as Lord Alderton's eyebrows lifted. "I have not heard much about it at all. Is it very far from London?"

Lord Alderton shook his head and smiled.

"No, it is not too far. Maybe a day or two's drive unless the road is particularly difficult. I have had some success with crop rotation these last few years." Chuckling, he shook his head. "I am sure that such things are not of any interest to you, however."

"No, indeed, I am always very interested in such matters, particularly if they concern an estate that I am one day to call my own."

She smiled warmly and took in the flash in Lord Alderton's eyes. He was the one who had mentioned betrothal, but now that *she* spoke of his estate as being her future home, he seemed a little taken aback.

"Yes, yes, of course."

He shrugged and smiled, his uneasy manner fading while Cassandra's doubts sprouted to truth. What Lord Alderton had told her, what he had confessed by way of his feelings - she was now sure that none of it was legitimate. He did not mean what he had said. He had never meant the words which he had spoken. No doubt he had said them simply to garner her affections, to make certain that she remained close to him – and after what she had said, the only way to keep her close was for her to believe that he cared for her.

And she might very well have believed it all, might have been convinced by it, had it not been for her thoughts continually turning to Lord Sherbourne... just as they were doing now.

Lord Alderton's gaze touched on something behind her, and a brief smile followed, though his brows knotted together.

"I shall leave you for the moment." Heaving a great sigh, he bowed toward her. "No doubt you will have many other gentlemen seeking to write their name upon your dance card, even *if* I might disapprove." Grimacing, he let his gaze fix on hers, his severe look lingering. "However, I look forward to dancing the waltz with you, Lady Cassandra. It will be one of my greatest joys."

Cassandra fought hard to remain precisely where she was and not look over her shoulder. As much as she wanted to, it would be best for her to keep her expression calm, to smile and nod in return.

"I look forward to it also, Lord Alderton."

With another brief smile, she watched him as he turned, moving away from her quickly. The reason for his departure soon became clear, as a familiar voice reached her ears.

"You have spoken to him then."

Lord Sherbourne moved towards her, and Cassandra's heart leaped.

"Yes, I have. He has stepped away, telling me that I will be inundated with gentlemen wishing to dance with me."

She laughed and rolled her eyes but Lord Sherbourne only smiled.

"In that regard I believe he is quite correct." Lord Sherbourne took her hand from the moment he looked into her face. His voice was suddenly lower, suddenly softer, and a frisson of excitement ran through Cassandra's frame. "You do know how highly I think of you, Cassandra."

Cassandra did not miss the familiar way that he spoke her name. The touch of his hand on hers made everything within her turn to light. She did not want to look away from him, could not bring herself to turn even a little away. Instead, her heart demanded that she move closer, although they were in full view of everyone else in the ballroom.

"I feel much the same, Lord Sherbourne." Her throat constricted for a moment. "When this is at an end, there is more I desire to share with you." Her voice softened as she lowered it to a mere whisper, wanting no one else to hear her words but him. "I have not told you everything which is in my heart."

A gentle fire lit his eyes as he smiled.

"I believe you and I find ourselves in much the same position, then." His fingers pressed hers once more, before he moved back, making a space between them that she wished was not there. "Now, might I have your dance card? If you should like to dance with me, that is."

"I should be very glad to."

Quickly handing her dance card to him, she watched as he wrote his name first in one place and then another. The smile which lit his features seemed to be filled with mirth over something she did not yet understand.

"He will forgive me, I hope."

"What have you done?" Taking her dance card back, Cassandra studied it for a moment, only for her eyes to flare and a tinkling laugh to break. Lord Sherbourne had written his name over the top of Lord Alderton's, meaning that *he* was the one she would stand up with for the waltz. Lifting her eyes, Cassandra made to reach for him, only to pull her hand back, worried that someone would notice her response. "It seems as though Lord Alderton is never to have his waltz." So saying with a great pretense of sadness, she shook her head. "Not that I should mind. I had no intention of standing up with him anyway."

Lord Sherbourne grinned.

"All the same, I am glad to have taken it from him, just to be sure that it is secured."

It seemed that he was bold where she was not, for his hand reached out and his fingers brushed her cheek. His touch was there for just a moment and then gone the next, making her heart burn with such a fury, she had to catch her breath.

"Good heavens, Lord Sherbourne, do you have intentions of giving our plan away before it is time?"

Before either Cassandra or Lord Sherbourne could react, Lady Yardley came to stand directly between them, her hand reaching up to push Lord Sherbourne's hand away from Cassandra's cheek.

"There will be time for such things later, but the moment is almost upon us. Are you quite prepared??"

Her eyes swiveled to Cassandra, who nodded.

"Yes. You have received the publication?"

While Lady Yardley smiled, there was no light to her eyes but an expression of seriousness lingered.

"Yes, I have. Your friends each have a copy."

Cassandra swallowed, the edge of nervousness tickling in her throat. There was a good deal at stake, and she had to play this out well. Thankfully, there was no concern that her reputation would be damaged – and even if there had been, Cassandra was sure that she had Lord Sherbourne's affection. No one else's consideration of her seemed to matter.

"Go to Lord Alderton," Lady Yardley instructed. "Your friends will be watching, ready to step nearer to Lord Alderton when required – just as you yourself suggested."

"Thank you." There was a hint of anxiousness about what she was to do, but with it came the confidence that, as she did so, the truth about Lord Alderton and what it was, precisely, that he wanted from her would be revealed. "I am prepared." Smiling first at her cousin, she then looked to Lord Sherbourne, reaching out one hand to him. "Will you wish me good luck?"

Lord Sherbourne grasped her hand, bending over it as he spoke.

"I do not think you have any requirement for luck," he told her, his eyes once more fixing on hers. "You will do marvelously well, Lady Cassandra, as you do all things – and I am very much looking forward to dancing the waltz with you, knowing that you are free of Lord Alderton for good."

"And that the other young ladies of London will be aware of the need to avoid him also." Lady Yardley glanced around the room. "This is done not only for your sake,

Cassandra, but also so that Lord Alderton's true character might be shown to the *ton*. Then, I assure you that anything written in 'The London Ledger' will not be rumor, but the truth, and he will have nothing to say for that."

Aware of the responsibility that she was being handed, Cassandra took a deep breath, set her shoulders, and lifted her chin.

"I shall go to him now."

Without so much as another word, she turned away from both Lord Sherbourne and her cousin and set out in search of Lord Alderton.

"Lord Alderton, there you are."

The gentleman in question had not taken her too long to find. He was ensconced in a corner of the room, speaking to two young ladies, who then took their leave of him as Cassandra approached.

"Lady Cassandra."

His hand went to her, and she took it, grasping it tightly, hoping that the fear she put into her voice would evidence itself in her eyes.

"Lord Alderton, I must beg of you – do not read 'The London Ledger'!"

Lord Alderton frowned immediately.

"'The London Ledger'?" he repeated, clearly confused. "Whatever are you speaking of, Lady Cassandra? We are at a ball, there cannot be such a thing here."

Closing her eyes, Cassandra, let out a long breath, clenching her jaw tightly so that she shuddered lightly.

"And yet, someone has brought a few copies of it here and I have seen some young ladies reading it!" Opening her eyes, she moved a few steps backward, as though in painful distress while intentionally making certain that a few more guests nearby in the ballroom might hear them. Lady Yardley, Lord Sherbourne, and her friends would be close by, also, ready to take in Lord Alderton's words, ready to step forward if it was required. "I do not know how it has been discovered." Taking in Lord Alderton's now widened eyes, she let out a choked exclamation. "You must not- I pray that you will not –"

Lord Alderton drew closer.

"Lady Cassandra, whatever is troubling you, I beg of you to share it with me. You appear most distressed."

"That is because I *am* distressed," she wailed, garnering the attention of a few more within the room. "To be written about in such a manner when our connection has only just been solidified, when you have been speaking of courtship and betrothal... I am beyond horrified. I assure you, even *I* did not know of this."

It was with satisfaction that she watched Lord Alderton's gaze now rove around the room. In one swift movement, he released her hand, stepped to the side, and snatched 'The London Ledger' from someone nearby – which, Cassandra noted, was none other than Lady Almira. She, of course, made no word of protest but rather offered Cassandra a brief nod.

Lord Alderton stood precisely where he was, scanning through the paper, his eyes going to every line. Cassandra knew the moment that he saw it, for his face froze in a startled expression, his eyes wide, color draining from his face. Cassandra herself clasped her hands to her heart in what she hoped was both a sorrowful and yet shocked expression.

"I swear to you that I did not know."

She moved forward quickly, glad to see now that Lord

Alderton was standing a little more within the room. There were a good many more people to hear him, and such was his shock, his voice was unguarded, his words loud enough for many of the nearby guests to hear.

"You have no dowry."

The darkness of his eyes and his expression sent a genuine shudder through Cassandra's frame.

"That is not precisely what it says," she implored, reaching out for him again as Lord Alderton shook his head and took a small step back. "It says I have a little but it will be a good deal less than that of my sister."

"But the generosity of your father with your sister's dowry was well known." Lord Alderton shook his head, then smacked at the paper with his free hand. "This is not what I expected, particularly when you *yourself* told Lord Darlington that you expected to have much the same dowry as your sister."

"But I did not know for certain," Cassandra explained, now overwhelmingly relieved that, in one sentence Lord Alderton had proven himself to be just as Lord Sherbourne had expected. He had no genuine feeling for her, no real interest. Instead, all he cared for was the dowry that she would bring with her, and thus he would do anything to satisfy her.

"This is beyond comprehension." Lord Alderton shook his head furiously. "A gentleman cannot be expected to commit himself to a lady whose father offers such a small reward for taking her off his hands."

Lifting an eyebrow, Cassandra took a small step towards him, ready to throw back something just as sharp, just as cutting, only to recall that she was meant to be greatly distressed by Lord Alderton's manner. Quickly, she lowered her head.

"But surely such a thing does not matter, Lord Alderton? Not when you have, only a few days ago, declared yourself to have a gentle affection for me." Keeping her voice as soft as she dared, she lifted her head and looked directly at him, but Lord Alderton was doing his best to look anywhere but her eyes. "Lord Alderton, *please* do not step back from me! You told me that you cared for me, you spoke of betrothal. You know very well that I wanted to marry a gentleman to whom I could offer my heart. Surely you will not step away from me now! You will not put away our happy connection, will not ignore the love which has begun to blossom, all for the sake of my dowry... or lack thereof."

"I care nothing for your heart." Lord Alderton's face was now a scarlet red, his lips curling into a sneer as he dismissed her with one sharp wave of his hand. "A dowry as significant as your sister's is all that I required from you. You asked about my estate and what I did *not* tell you is that there are a great many repairs being undertaken. Where do you think the money for such repairs has come from? Despite my attempts at crop rotation, the results have been poor, but all must continue if my house is to stay standing. I require a wife with a substantial dowry and a yearly income from a generous father - and I thought that you would bring both of those into our marriage."

Before Cassandra could say anything in response, Lady Yardley moved forward, striding towards Cassandra so that she stood beside her. It was only then that Cassandra realized just how many onlookers there were, how many were listening to this particular conversation. Her own face flashed hot, praying that her cousin would say something to make those who watched aware that this was nothing but a pretense on Cassandra's part.

"Well, Lord Alderton, it seems that the truth about your

character has been revealed to us all." Lady Yardley gestured to those who watched and Lord Alderton's color which had become raised during his outburst, quickly began to drain away. "You are aware, of course, that *I* am the one who owns 'The London Ledger'. *I* decide what is written within it, and when Cassandra's concerns grew over your behavior and conduct, she thought it best to make certain that your attentions to her – your professions of love and affection and your promise of betrothal – were exactly as they appeared to be." She took Cassandra's arm. "All of this was Cassandra's doing, and I am heartily relieved to know that she has saved herself from a gentleman such as you. Have no doubt, Lord Alderton, *this* evening's shocking confessions which have fallen from your lips will be written in 'The London Ledger'. Your response to hearing the suggestion that my cousin may not have as significant a dowry as you hoped for is one that all of society shall know of. They will hear of your promises of affection and betrothal – and thereafter, shall hear of how poorly you have treated her. I am only glad that she has no genuine affection for you. This was nothing more than a test, Lord Alderton – a test which you have failed."

Lord Sherbourne moved to her side and before he could even offer it, she had taken his arm.

"And lest you have actually spread any of those rumors you spoke of, let me make it known that *you* placed that diamond bracelet in Lord Sherbourne's pocket." Lady Yardley spoke as though it were a fact rather than a question, gesturing to Lord Sherbourne as she did so. "You saw that he was becoming close with Lady Cassandra, and thought to ruin him – or at least, to hold the threat of ruination over his head. You did not want him to have any nearness to Lady Cassandra, so that she would turn only to you – and all in the hope of gaining her dowry."

"And I have written in the Ledger that *I* am the one who found the bracelet. Whoever comes forward, they will not blame Lord Sherbourne. Your plans have failed, Lord Alderton. Perhaps you yourself are the thief."

Given how Lord Alderton responded to this – his face burning hot at her statement – Cassandra had every reason to believe that it was as she had suggested. Once more, Lord Alderton had proven himself *not* to be the gentleman she had thought him.

"I think that our conversation is at an end." Cassandra spoke firmly, her eyebrows lifting as Lord Alderton dropped his head low "There shall not be any courtship between us, Lord Alderton. I am not inclined to tie myself to a gentleman who lies, who pretends to feel all manner of things simply to gain a little more wealth for himself. Regardless of your reasons for doing so, I have no interest in spending even one further minute of my time with you."

"An excellent ending." Lord Sherbourne smiled, his eyes bright and as vivid as she had remembered them. "Mayhap you will be willing to walk with me, Lady Cassandra, before the waltz begins?"

Free of all fear, trepidation, confusion, and doubt, Cassandra smiled at him, her heart filled with a great and overwhelming affection that she knew could only be the promise of love.

"I can think of nothing I would like more," she murmured, before taking his arm and stepping away.

EPILOGUE

*A*ll Jonathan could hear was the thunder of his heartbeat in his ears, the sound drowning out every other noise as he made his way into the drawing-room where he hoped Lady Cassandra was waiting. It had been two days since the altercation with Lord Alderton, two days where he had learned exactly what Lord Alderton was seeking, and two days since he had realized just how much he longed to take Lady Cassandra into his arms again. If she had ended up being courted by Lord Alderton, Jonathan did not know what state he would have been in at present. No doubt he would have been a vague shadow of himself, lost, stumbling, confused in the darkness, not knowing where he was to go. He would now be walking about, his heart filled with nothing but regret over his lack of honesty within his own heart and sorrow over what he had lost. To be given another opportunity now was wonderful, and one which he intended to grasp hold of, trusting that he would never let her go.

"Lord Sherbourne."

She spoke his name with a warmth that filled Jonathan's

heart with overwhelming heat, his gaze settling on her. How could he have ever stood by and allowed her to be on the arm of another gentleman? How foolish he had been to not see the significance of what was within his heart before now!

"My dear Cassandra."

With a softness to his voice, he held out one hand and she gave him hers just as willingly, rising from her chair. It was only when Lady Yardley also rose, that Jonathan realized they were not alone. All the same, he dropped Lady Cassandra's hand and inclined his head, keenly aware of Lady Yardley's broad smile.

"Did you know that the diamond bracelet has been returned to its owner?"

Lady Yardley's smile lingered as Jonathan lifted his eyebrows in surprise.

"No, I had not heard. That was rather quick, was it not?"

"A young lady by the name of Miss Kinsley appeared with her mother, Lady Dutton." Lady Cassandra giggled suddenly, her eyes flashing brightly. "Apparently she had worn the diamond bracelet without her mother's permission, and was now deeply ashamed that she had lost it."

Lady Yardley chuckled alongside her cousin.

"I do not know who was more relieved, the mother or the daughter!"

Letting out a slow breath of relief, Jonathan joined in the mirth, smiling first at Lady Yardley and then looking to Lady Cassandra, letting his gaze stay there. His thoughts lingered on just how beautiful she was, how much joy she brought to his heart, and how much he wished to give all of himself to her.

"I am very glad to hear that it has been returned."

"And it seems as though Lord Alderton has left London and gone back to his estate." Lady Cassandra's smile faltered for a moment. "I will confess myself a little ashamed to have been taken in by him."

"Nonsense." Lady Yardley settled one hand on Lady Cassandra's shoulder. "You were cautious, and you were careful and what is more, you listened to your heart." Her eyes slid towards Jonathan. "And that, I think, is the most important thing. Would you not agree, Lord Sherbourne?"

With no hesitation, Jonathan nodded.

"Yes, indeed, I would."

He spoke not to Lady Yardley but to Lady Cassandra. Her eyes glowed softly, her small smile setting her expression alight. Lady Yardley nodded as though she were quite satisfied, and then immediately turned towards the door, murmuring to Jonathan that she would only give him a few minutes and she hoped that it would be enough.

Jonathan did not move, relieved that Lady Yardley trusted him, but also grateful to her for her absence. He did not wait for even an instant, and thus the moment that Lady Yardley left the room, he stepped forward and caught both of Lady Cassandra's hands with his own.

"I have searched my heart also." His heart began to pound as she smiled gently, his desire to be honest with her overflowing with such strength that he could not prevent the rush of words from continuing. "And I think that I must beg for your forgiveness."

Lady Cassandra's eyes flared.

"Forgiveness?"

Jonathan nodded.

"Had I been honest with myself, then I might well have had the courage to be honest with you also. Then matters with Lord Alderton might not have taken the turn that they did, and you might have been spared a great deal of trouble."

Lady Cassandra's surprise faded into a gentle smile.

"But Lord Sherbourne, had I not gone through such a trial, then perhaps I would not have recognized what is within my own heart." She moved closer, freeing one hand so that she might press it against his cheek. "At the beginning, I was confused and troubled by all that I felt whenever you were in the same room as I. I ignored my feelings, set them aside, pushed them away, telling myself that Lord Alderton was the best choice of gentleman, just so long as he could find himself in love with me. I knew that you did not ascribe value to the notion of love and, while you mayhap did not think me foolish, you were not seeking a love match. Therefore, I told myself that it was best to pretend I felt nothing."

Giving a small nod of understanding, Jonathan allowed himself to brush his fingers at her temple, the softness of her skin under his fingertips a sensation he had been longing to feel. It was just as wonderful as he had imagined.

"For many years I have told myself that practicality was all that was required when it came to my future bride. I believed that having a wife would bring an extra burden, an extra responsibility to the title I already bore. I never once thought that a wife might be more of a blessing than a weight, that she might be able to lessen the burden which I carry rather than add to it. I did not let myself even dream of how much beauty and joy such a lady might bring into my life. But now, as I stand here before you, I can see my future – and it is filled with light, filled with all of the things which I did not ever even dream about. It is a light which only *you* bring, Cassandra."

"And I am at peace now that my heart is free to tell you

how much I love you, Sherbourne." Her soft words were a solace to Jonathan's heart, bringing a fresh sense of joy and completeness, that he had never once experienced in his life before. "I was waiting for my heart to draw itself towards Lord Alderton but it simply refused to do so." Again, her hand reached to his cheek, running lightly across his skin before going around his neck. "It had already drawn itself to someone else entirely."

Jonathan's heart quickened.

"And I am honored that you should choose me." His hands went to her waist, drawing her close to him. "It brings me great joy to say that I love you too, Cassandra."

For some moments, they simply looked into each other's eyes, enjoying the sweetness of what had been shared between them. The words which had been spoken settled into Jonathan, his heart flooding with a deep and over-flowing love for the young lady he held in his arms. When he lowered his head, she was waiting for him, ready with her kiss. It was with a great effort that Jonathan held back the desire which plunged through him as he took her into his arms, allowing their kiss to be only brief, and yet so very sweet, speaking of a promise which they might each cling to – a hope that their future would be just as beautiful and as contented as this one moment. All he had to do was to make sure that she knew of his love with every single day that passed between them.

"I think I shall have to write to your father." Lady Cassandra laughed softly as Jonathan barely pulled himself back, unwilling to end the kiss, but having more to say. "My desire for you is true. My intentions for you are honorable. I want to make you my bride so that I might tell you every day how much I love you."

Lady Cassandra's eyes were still closed, but her smile was beautiful.

"I will love you for the rest of my life," she whispered as Jonathan kissed her again, lightly. "Our love is true and everlasting, and the strength of it will bind us together for the rest of our days."

I AM glad Lady Cassandra and Jonathan were able to finally get together! They make a great couple.

Preorder the next book in the Only for Love series!

In a world of secrets and scandal, Miss Bridget Wynch unknowingly threatens Lord Landon's hidden past, forcing him to decide between love and the truth that could tear them apart.

Preorder here A Lord or a Liar

Need something to read now? Check out the first book of the Ladies on their Own series.

MY DEAR READER

Thank you for reading and supporting my books! I hope this story brought you some escape from the real world into the always captivating Regency world. A good story, especially one with a happy ending, just brightens your day and makes you feel good! If you enjoyed the book, would you leave a review on Amazon? Reviews are always appreciated.

Below is a complete list of all my books! Why not click and see if one of them can keep you entertained for a few hours?

The Returned Lords of Grosvenor Square
The Returned Lords of Grosvenor Square: A Regency
Romance Boxset
The Waiting Bride
The Long Return
The Duke's Saving Grace
A New Home for the Duke

The Spinsters Guild
The Spinsters Guild: A Sweet Regency Romance Boxset
A New Beginning
The Disgraced Bride
A Gentleman's Revenge
A Foolish Wager
A Lord Undone

Convenient Arrangements
Convenient Arrangements: A Regency Romance
Collection
A Broken Betrothal
In Search of Love
Wed in Disgrace
Betrayal and Lies
A Past to Forget
Engaged to a Friend

Landon House
Landon House: A Regency Romance Boxset
Mistaken for a Rake
A Selfish Heart
A Love Unbroken
A Christmas Match
A Most Suitable Bride

An Expectation of Love

Second Chance Regency Romance
Second Chance Regency Romance Boxset
Loving the Scarred Soldier
Second Chance for Love
A Family of her Own
A Spinster No More

Soldiers and Sweethearts
To Trust a Viscount
Whispers of the Heart
Dare to Love a Marquess
Healing the Earl
A Lady's Brave Heart

Ladies on their Own: Governesses and Companions
Ladies on their Own Boxset
More Than a Companion
The Hidden Governess
The Companion and the Earl
More than a Governess
Protected by the Companion

Lost Fortunes, Found Love
A Viscount's Stolen Fortune
For Richer, For Poorer
Her Heart's Choice
A Dreadful Secret
Their Forgotten Love
His Convenient Match

Only for Love

The Heart of a Gentleman
A Lord or a Liar

Christmas Stories
Love and Christmas Wishes: Three Regency Romance
Novellas
A Family for Christmas
Mistletoe Magic: A Regency Romance
Heart, Homes & Holidays: A Sweet Romance Anthology

Happy Reading!
All my love,
Rose

A SNEAK PEEK OF MORE
THAN A COMPANION

"*D*id you hear me, Honora?"

Miss Honora Gregory lifted her head at once, knowing that her father did not refer to her as 'Honora' very often and that he only did so when he was either irritated or angry with her.

"I do apologize, father, I was lost in my book," Honora replied, choosing to be truthful with her father rather than make excuses, despite the ire she feared would now follow. "Forgive my lack of consideration."

This seemed to soften Lord Greene just a little, for his scowl faded and his lips were no longer taut.

"I shall only repeat myself the once," her father said firmly, although there was no longer that hint of frustration in his voice. "There is very little money, Nora. I cannot give you a Season."

All thought of her book fled from Honora's mind as her eyes fixed to her father's, her chest suddenly tight. She had known that her father was struggling financially, although she had never been permitted to be aware of the details. But not to have a Season was deeply upsetting, and Honora had to immediately fight back hot tears which sprang into her eyes. There had always been a little hope in her heart, had always been a flicker of expectation that, despite knowing her father's situation, he might still be able to take her to London."

"Your aunt, however, is eager to go to London," Lord Greene continued, as Honora pressed one hand to her stomach in an attempt to soothe the sudden rolling and writhing which had captured her. He waved a hand dismissively, his expression twisting. "I do not know the reasons for it, given that she is widowed and, despite that, happily settled, but it seems she is determined to have some time in London this summer. Therefore, whilst you are not to have a Season of your own – you will not be presented or the like – you will go with your aunt to London."

Honora swallowed against the tightness in her throat, her hands twisting at her gown as she fought against a myriad of emotions.

"I am to be her companion?" she said, her voice only just a whisper as her father nodded.

She had always been aware that Lady Langdon, her aunt, had only ever considered her own happiness and her own situation, but to invite your niece to London as your companion rather than chaperone her for a Season surely spoke of selfishness!

"It is not what you might have hoped for, I know," her father continued, sounding resigned as a small sigh escaped his lips, his shoulders slumping. Honora looked up at him, seeing him now a little grey and realizing the full extent of his weariness. Some of her upset faded as she took in her father's demeanor, knowing that his lack of financial security was not his doing. The estate lands had done poorly these last three years, what with drought one year and flooding the next. As such, money had been ploughed into the ground to restore it and yet it would not become profitable again for at least another year. She could not blame her father for that. And yet, her heart had struggled against such news, trying to be glad that she would be in London but broken-hearted to learn that her aunt wanted her as her companion and nothing more. "I will not join you, of course," Lord Greene continued, coming a little closer to Honora and tilting his head just a fraction, studying his daughter carefully and, perhaps, all too aware of her inner turmoil. "You can, of course, choose to refuse your aunt's invitation – but I can offer you nothing more than what is being given to you at present, Nora. This may be your only opportunity to be in London."

Honora blinked rapidly against the sudden flow of hot tears that threatened to pour from her eyes, should she permit them.

"It is very good of my aunt," she managed to say, trying to be both gracious and thankful whilst ignoring the other, more negative feelings which troubled her. "Of course, I shall go."

Lord Greene smiled sadly, then reached out and settled one hand on Honora's shoulder, bending down just a little as he did so.

"My dear girl, would that I could give you more. You already have enough to endure, with the loss of your mother when you were just a child yourself. And now you have a poor father who cannot provide for you as he ought."

"I understand, Father," Honora replied quickly, not wanting to have her father's soul laden with guilt. "Pray, do not concern yourself. I shall be contented enough with what Lady Langdon has offered me."

Her father closed his eyes and let out another long sigh, accompanied this time with a shake of his head.

"She may be willing to allow you a little freedom, my dear girl," he said, without even the faintest trace of hope in his voice. "My sister has always been inclined to think only of herself, but there may yet be a change in her character."

Honora was still trying to accept the news that she was to be a companion to her aunt and could not make even a murmur of agreement. She closed her eyes, seeing a vision of herself standing in a ballroom, surrounded by ladies and gentlemen of the *ton*. She could almost hear the music, could almost feel the warmth on her skin... and then realized that she would be sitting quietly at the back of the room, able only to watch, and not to engage with any of it. Pain etched itself across her heart and Honora let out a long, slow breath, allowing the news to sink into her very soul.

"Thank you, Father." Her voice was hoarse but her words heartfelt, knowing that her father was doing his very best for her in the circumstances. "I will be a good companion for my aunt."

"I am sure that you will be, my dear," he said, quietly. "And I will pray that, despite everything, you might find a match – even in the difficulties that face us."

The smile faded from Honora's lips as, with that, her father left the room. There was very little chance of such a thing happening, as she was to be a companion rather than a debutante. The realization that she would be an afterthought, a lady worth nothing more than a mere glance from the moment that she set foot in London, began to tear away at Honora's heart, making her brow furrow and her lips pull downwards. There could be no moments of sheer enjoyment for her, no time when she was not considering all that was required of her as her aunt's companion. She would have to make certain that her thoughts were always fixed on her responsibilities, that her intentions were settled on her aunt at all times. Yes, there would be gentlemen to smile at and, on the rare chance, mayhap even converse with, but her aunt would not often permit such a thing, she was sure. Lady Langdon had her own reasons for going to London for the Season, whatever they were, and Honora was certain she would take every moment for herself.

"I must be grateful," Honora murmured to herself, setting aside her book completely as she rose from her chair and meandered towards the window.

Looking out at the grounds below, she took in the gardens, the pond to her right and the rose garden to her left. There were so many things here that held such beauty and, with it, such fond memories that there was a part of her, Honora had to admit, which did not want to leave it, did not want to set foot in London where she might find herself in a new and lower situation. There was security here, a comfort which encouraged her to remain, which told her to hold fast to all that she knew – but Honora was all too aware that she could not. Her future was not here. When her father passed away, if she was not wed, then Honora knew that she would be left to continue on as a companion, just to make certain that she had a home and enough coin for her later years. That was not the future she wanted but, she considered, it might very well be all that she could gain. Tears began to swell in her eyes, and she dropped her head, squeezing her eyes closed and forcing the tears back. This was the only opportunity she would have to go to London and, whilst it was not what she had hoped for, Honora had to accept it for what it was and begin to prepare herself for leaving her father's house – possibly, she considered, for good. Clasping both hands together, Honora drew in a long breath and let it out slowly as her eyes closed and her shoulders dropped.

A new part of her life was beginning. A new and unexpected future was being offered to her, and Honora had no other choice but to grasp it with both hands.

$\mathcal{P}$ushing all doubt aside, Robert walked into White's with the air of someone who expected not only to be noticed, but to be greeted and exclaimed over in the most exaggerated manner. His chin lifted as he snapped his fingers towards one of the waiting footmen, giving him his request for the finest of brandies in short, sharp words. Then, he continued to make his way inside, his hands swinging loosely by his sides, his shoulders pulled back and his chest a little puffed out.

"Goodness, is that you?"

Robert grinned, his expectations seeming to be met, as a gentleman to his left rose to his feet and came towards him, only for him to stop suddenly and shake his head.

"Forgive me, you are not Lord Johnstone," he said, holding up both hands, palms out, towards Robert. "I thought that you were he, for you have a very similar appearance."

Grimacing, Robert shrugged and said not a word, making his way past the gentleman and finding a slight heat rising into his face. To be mistaken for another was one thing, but to remain entirely unrecognized was quite another! His doubts attempted to come rushing back. Surely someone would remember him, would remember what he had done last Season?

"Lord Crampton, good evening."

Much to his relief, Robert heard his title being spoken and turned his head to the right, seeing a gentleman sitting in a high-backed chair, a glass of brandy in his hand and a small smile on his face as he looked up at Robert.

"Good evening, Lord Marchmont," Robert replied, glad indeed that someone, at least, had recognized him. "I am back in London, as you can see."

"I hope you find it a pleasant visit," came the reply, only for Lord Marchmont to turn away and continue speaking to another gentleman sitting opposite – a man whom Robert had neither seen, nor was acquainted with. There was no suggestion from Lord Marchmont about introducing Robert to him and, irritated, Robert turned sharply away. His head dropped, his shoulders rounded, and he did not even attempt to keep his frustration out of his expression. His jaw tightened, his eyes blazed and his hands balled into fists.

Had they all forgotten him so quickly?

Practically flinging himself into a large, overstuffed armchair in the corner of White's, Robert began to mutter darkly to himself, almost angry about how he had been treated. Last Season he had been the talk of London! Why should he be so easily forgotten now? Unpleasant memories rose, of being inconspicuous, and disregarded, when he had first inherited his title. He attempted to push them aside, but his upset grew steadily so that even the brandy he was given by the footman – who had spent some minutes trying to find Lord Crampton – tasted like ash in his mouth. Nothing took his upset away and Robert wrapped it around his shoulders like a blanket, huddling against it and keeping it close to him.

He had not expected this. He had hoped to be not only remembered but celebrated! When he stepped into a room, he thought that he should be noticed. He *wanted* his name to be murmured by others, for it to be spread around the room that he had arrived! Instead, he was left with an almost painful frustration that he had been so quickly forgotten by the *ton* who, only a few months ago, had been his adoring admirers.

"Another brandy might help remove that look from your face." Robert did not so much as blink, hearing the man's voice but barely acknowledging it. "You are upset, I can tell." The man rose and came to sit opposite Robert, who finally was forced to recognize him. "That is no way for a gentleman to appear upon his first few days in London!"

Robert's lip curled. He should not, he knew, express his frustration so openly, but he found that he could not help himself.

"Good evening, Lord Burnley," he muttered, finding the man's broad smile and bright eyes to be nothing more than an irritation. "Are *you* enjoying the London Season thus far?"

Lord Burnley chuckled, his eyes dancing - which added to Robert's irritation all the more. He wanted to turn his head away, to make it plain to Lord Burnley that he did not enjoy his company and wanted very much to be free of it, but his standing as a gentleman would not permit him to do so.

"I have only been here a sennight but yes, I have found

a great deal of enjoyment thus far," Lord Burnley told him. "But you should expect that, should you not? After all, a gentleman coming to London for the Season comes for good company, fine wine, excellent conversation and to be in the company of beautiful young ladies – one of whom might even catch his eye!"

This was, of course, suggestive of the fact that Lord Burnley might have had his head turned already by one of the young women making their come out, but Robert was in no mood to enter such a discussion. Instead, he merely sighed, picked up his glass again and held it out to the nearby footman, who came over to them at once.

"Another," he grunted, as the man took his glass from him. "And for Lord Burnley here."

Lord Burnley chuckled again, the sound grating on Robert's skin.

"I am quite contented with what I have at present, although I thank you for your consideration," he replied, making Robert's brow lift in surprise. What sort of gentleman turned down the opportunity to drink fine brandy? Half wishing that Lord Burnley would take his leave so that he might sit here in silence and roll around in his frustration, Robert settled back in his chair, his arms crossed over his chest and his gaze turned away from Lord Burnley in the vain hope that this would encourage the man to take his leave. He realized that he was behaving churlishly, yet somehow, he could not prevent it – he had hoped so much, and so far, nothing was as he had expected. "So, you are returned to London," Lord Burnley said, making Robert roll his eyes at the ridiculous observation which, for whatever reason, Lord Burnley either did not notice or chose to ignore. "Do you have any particular intentions for this Season?"

Sending a lazy glance towards Lord Burnley, Robert shrugged.

"If you mean to ask whether or not I intend to pursue one particular young lady with the thought of matrimony in mind, then I must tell you that you are mistaken to even *think* that I should care for such a thing," he stated, plainly. "I am here only to enjoy myself."

"I see."

Lord Burnley gave no comment in judgment of Robert's statement, but Robert felt it nonetheless, quite certain that Lord Burnley now thought less of him for being here solely for his own endeavors. He scowled. Lord Burnley might have decided that it was the right time for him to wed, but Robert had no intention of doing so whatsoever. Given his good character, given his standing and his title, there would be very few young ladies who would suit him, and Robert knew that it would take a significant effort not only to first identify such a young lady but also to then make certain that she would suit him completely. It was not something that he wanted to put his energy into at present. For the moment, Robert had every intention of simply dancing and conversing and mayhap even calling upon the young ladies of the *ton*, but that would be for his own enjoyment rather than out of any real consideration.

Besides which, he told himself, *given that the* ton *will, no doubt, remember all that you did last Season, there will be many young ladies seeking out your company which would make it all the more difficult to choose only one, should you have any inclination to do so!*

"And are you to attend Lord Newport's ball tomorrow evening?"

Being pulled from his thoughts was an irritating interruption and Robert let the long sigh fall from his lips without hesitation, sending it in Lord Burnley's direction who, much to Robert's frustration, did not even react to it.

"I am," Robert replied, grimacing. "Although I do hope that the other guests will not make too much of my arrival. I should not like to steal any attention away from Lord and Lady Newport."

Allowing himself a few moments of study, Robert looked back at Lord Burnley and waited to see if there was even a hint of awareness in his expression. Lord Burnley, however, merely shrugged one shoulder and turned his head away, making nothing at all of what Robert had told him. Gritting his teeth, Robert closed his eyes and tried to force out another long, calming breath. He did not need Lord Burnley to remember what he had done, nor to celebrate it. What was important was that the ladies of the *ton* recalled it, for then he would be more than certain to have their attention for the remainder of the Season – and that was precisely what Robert wanted. Their attention would elevate him in the eyes of the *ton*, would bring him into sharp relief against the other gentlemen who were enjoying the Season in London. He did not care what the gentlemen thought of him, he reminded himself, for their considerations were of no importance save for the fact that they might be able to invite him to various social occasions.

Robert's shoulders dropped and he opened his eyes. Coming to White's this evening had been a mistake. He ought to have made his way to some soiree or other, for he had many invitations already but, given that he had only arrived in London the day before, had thought it too early to make his entrance into society. That had been a mistake. The *ton* ought to know of his arrival just as soon as was possible, so that his name might begin to be whispered amongst them. He could not bear the idea that the pleasant notoriety he had experienced last Season might have faded already!

A small smile pulled at his lips as he considered this, his heart settling into a steady rhythm, free from frustration and upset now. Surely, it was not that he was not remembered by society, but rather that he had chosen the wrong place to make his entrance. The gentlemen of London would not make his return to society of any importance, given that they would be jealous and envious of his desirability in the eyes of the ladies of the *ton*, and therefore, he ought not to have expected such a thing from them! A quiet chuckle escaped his lips as Robert shook his head, passing one hand over his eyes for a moment. It had been a simple mistake and that mistake had brought him irritation and confusion – but that would soon be rectified, once he made his way into full London society.

"You appear to be in better spirits now, Lord Crampton."

Robert's brow lifted as he looked back at Lord Burnley, who was studying him with mild interest.

"I have just come to a realization," he answered, not wanting to go into a detailed explanation but at the same time, wanting to answer Lord Burnley's question. "I had hoped that I might have been greeted a little more warmly but, given my history, I realize now that I ought not to have expected it from a group of gentlemen."

Lord Burnley frowned.

"Your history?"

Robert's jaw tightened, wondering if it was truly that Lord Burnley did not know of what he spoke, or if he was saying such a thing simply to be a little irritating.

"You do not know?" he asked, his own brows drawing low over his eyes as he studied Lord Burnley's open expression. The man shook his head, his head tipping gently to one side in a questioning manner. "I am surprised. It was the talk of London!"

"Then I am certain you will be keen to inform me of it," Lord Burnley replied, his tone neither dull nor excited, making Robert's brow furrow all the more. "Was it something of significance?"

Robert gritted his teeth, finding it hard to believe that Lord Burnley, clearly present at last year's Season, did not know of what he spoke. For a moment, he thought he would not inform the fellow about it, given that he did not appear to be truly interested in what they spoke of, but then his pride won out and he began to explain.

"Are you acquainted with Lady Charlotte Fortescue?" he asked, seeing Lord Burnley shake his head. "She is the daughter of the Duke of Strathaven. Last Season, when I had only just stepped into the title of the Earl of Crampton, I discovered her being pulled away through Lord Kingsley's gardens by a most uncouth gentleman and, of course, in coming to her rescue, I struck the fellow a blow that had him knocked unconscious." His chin lifted slightly as he recalled that moment, remembering how Lady Charlotte had practically collapsed into his arms in the moments after he had struck the despicable Viscount Forthside and knocked him to the ground. Her father, the Duke of Strathaven, had been in search of his daughter and had found them both only a few minutes later, quickly followed by the Duchess of Strathaven. In fact, a small group of gentlemen and ladies had appeared in the gardens and had applauded him for his rescue – and news of it had quickly spread through London society. The Duke of Strathaven had been effusive in his appreciation and thankfulness for Robert's actions and Robert had reveled in it, finding that his newfound status within the *ton* was something to be enjoyed. He had assumed that it would continue into this Season and had told himself that, once he was at a ball or soiree with the ladies of the *ton*, his exaltation would continue. "The Duke and Duchess were, of course, very grateful," he finished, as Lord Burnley nodded slowly, although there was no exclamation of surprise on his lips nor a gasp of astonishment. "The gentlemen of London are likely a little envious of me, of course, but that is to be expected."

Much to his astonishment, Lord Burnley broke out into laughter at this statement, his eyes crinkling and his hand lifting his still-full glass towards Robert.

"Indeed, I am certain they are," he replied, his words filled with a sarcasm that could not be missed. "Good evening, Lord Crampton. I shall go now and tell the other gentlemen here in White's precisely who you are and what you have done. No doubt they shall come to speak to you at once, given your great and esteemed situation."

Robert set his jaw, his eyes a little narrowed as he watched Lord Burnley step away, all too aware of the man's cynicism. *It does not matter,* he told himself, firmly. *Lord Burnley, too, will be a little jealous of your success, and your standing in the* ton. *What else should you expect other than sarcasm and rebuttal?*

Rising to his feet, Robert set his shoulders and, with his head held high, made his way from White's, trying to ignore the niggle of doubt that entered his mind. Tomorrow, he told himself, he would find things much more improved. He would go to whatever occasion he wished and would find himself, of course, just as he had been last Season – practically revered by all those around him.

He could hardly wait.

CHECK out the rest of the story in the Kindle store! More Than a Companion

JOIN MY MAILING LIST

Sign up for my newsletter to stay up to date on new releases, contests, giveaways, freebies, and deals!

Free book with signup!

Monthly Facebook Giveaways! Books and Amazon gift cards!
Join me on Facebook: https://www.
facebook.com/rosepearsonauthor

Website: www.RosePearsonAuthor.com

Follow me on Goodreads: Author Page

Printed in Great Britain
by Amazon

26222252R00119